Eighteen Months

A screenplay written by
Leslie Jones McCloud

Eighteen Months
Copyright © 2008 by Leslie Jones McCloud
Gary, IN 46404
All rights reserved
ISBN: 978-0-6152-0992-0

Eighteen Months

Introduction

This screenplay is a work of fiction. It stems from a kept diary of my thoughts on being a crime reporter at the Chicago Defender Newspaper during the late1990s. I began to write my thoughts down during the year 2000, while taking the South Shore train in to Chicago (destination: 26 & California) to work as a police/courts reporter for the now defunct wire service, Alliance News. Please enjoy.

Leslie Jones McCloud

EIGHTEEN MONTHS

ACT I

FADE IN:

EXT: URBAN VACANT LOT-DAY

Men, women and children wander noisily around a vacant lot overgrown with weeds looking for a missing person.

The street is tree lined and littered with three-flats and single family dwellings.

A small crowd of 30 or so people in the hot July sun gathers near a thick patch of shrubs.

A woman's high-pitched scream breaks through the neighborhood noise. Hip-hop music is muted but playing in the background. Residents are vocal and alarmed that they have stumbled across the body of a man.

TOYMAN, the neighborhood success story, has finally been found--dead. Employees from his toy store run across the street to gawk at the man who gave many of them a chance to earn an honest living. Some of them weep openly.

Car loads of uniformed officers approach, and the crowd gives way. Police begin to rope off the area with yellow tape. Lead detectives VICTOR CROWE and THEO MARRSEC, stand over Toyman and twist their faces in disgust.

Crowe and Marrsec are mid career detectives who are rising stars in the police force because they have a 98 percent solvability rate on cases they investigate.

Toyman is laying mutilated in a thick patch of weeds. A bloody brick is nearby. Someone has tossed a dirty, blood-splattered sheet across his body.

> CROWE
> Not much we can do about this one, huh?

> MARRSEC
> Nope, not much at all.

Crowe, leaning over Toyman to closely examine the murder scene, notices a liquor bottle near his head. He picks it up and shoves it in his pocket.

News reporters stand among the crowd with pencils moving quickly. Others point cameras into the faces which make up the neighborhood.

On Crowe and Marrsec's direction, two men are led away and seated inside a squad car. The detectives seat themselves in the front seat of the car for only a moment. Then all of the men get out.

> CROWE
> They're okay.

Uniformed officers look confused but let the men go free. Crowe shoves something that looks like a roll of bills into his pocket.

One of the men lifts his bare arm in the direction of two little boys, pointing at them and nodding slowly.

Crowe signals to police to put the kids in the back of a police wagon.

A woman standing nearby starts to shriek and fight the police officers who carry out the task with grim looks on their faces. The crowd's grumbles grow louder.

A man picks up a baseball bat and shatters a police car's windshield. But he is quickly wrestled to the ground. Marrsec tries to calm the woman.

> MARRSEC
> Ma'am, we're just going to question the boys, that's all. They'll probably be home in time for dinner.
> Are you one of these boys' mother?

A man driving small dusty red car is parked across the street from the crowd, looking in the direction of the woman and Marrsec. The woman watches in silence as one of the four men inside turns his face towards hers and runs a gnarled finger across the front of his neck, signaling for the woman not to say a word.

Nervously, the woman rakes her thin fingers through uncombed hair, She is staring at detective Marrsec. They were both turned in the direction of the men but he did nothing more to assure her safety. Marrsec only returned her stare. The woman turns and runs up the stairs to an apartment inside.

INT. THREE FLAT-DAY

LOIS DUSOL, wobbles up a step stool, pregnant, and trying desperately to hang curtains up to her windows. She climbs down and looks at her effort. The curtains hang as lopsided as her life after surviving a failed marriage and a stalled career. The cordless phone hanging in the pocket of her housecoat rings.

>   LOIS
> Yes. Oh, I'd be happy to start next month. No, I'm
> due any day now so I'll be ready for any assignment
> you give me.. No, the police beat is fine.

Lois hangs up the phone satisfied. She then turns her attention to the television where a newscaster announces that police are searching for leads in the murder of Toyman.

INSERT TELEVISION NEWS ANNOUNCER:

"Police have called off their search for a local man who was reported missing last week..."

BACK TO SCENE

Lois soon goes back to hanging curtains, then stops long enough to fish a small pencil out of her pocket and write down the victim's name.

INT. OFFICE RECEP AREA-DAY TWO MONTHS LATER

Martin Combs doesn't like to lose. He is an ambitious and studious man known to friends simply as MC.

He enters the office suite he shares with Sydney Marrow, who is MC's law partner. The men are well respected, popular and comfortable. And somewhat self-absorbed.

MC shuffles through mail laying on the receptionist's desk then moves on to another task. He dashes yesterday's coffee into a nearby potted plant. He heads out of the office to the restroom with the coffee pot in his hand.

He sees the building's maintenance man Sal, scrubbing urinals.

INT. BATHROOM

          MC
Hey Sal. Nice day out huh?

Sal doesn't respond.

          MC
Hey, should I cut this?

MC rubs his mustache and starts to swish water around inside the coffee pot. The steam clouds the mirror. MC wipes away the steam and looks in the mirror at SAL, Who was busy scrubbing the insides of a urinal. He didn't stop scrubbing or bother to look up.

The jangle of his heavy key ring draped off of his hip echoed inside the bathroom. MC turned around and looked at the man.

          SAL
Uhdunno. What's wrong with it?

The man kept scrubbing, moving on to the next urinal.

          MC
Nothing, I guess. Just looking for a change. Anyway, thanks for installing the Jacuzzi. You gave me a pretty good deal on it. I sent the check out this morning.

MC rubbed his manicured, fingers slowly around his mustache, smoothing it down.

Looking at Sal's reflection in the mirror, he, for the first time, saw what Sal was doing. The sound of rustling paper, water sloshing, keys jangling and flushing filled the bathroom.

He noticed a thick hunch forming on Sal's shoulders and sweat was running into his eyes.

He looked at the sweaty, hunched over man and then his own hands and pinky ring.

>			MC
> How old are you, Sal?

>			SAL
> I'll be 35 next week.

>			MC
> Damn, Sal. We're the same age. I didn't know that.

>			SAL
> Yup, Sal replied. Time sure does fly-even when you ain't havin' fun.

>			SAL
> Let me know if you need anymore work done.

MC nodded and swished hot water around in the coffee pot then went back to looking in the mirror at himself. Then he closes his eyes tightly and splashes a little water on his face.

(His heartbeat is audible)

MONTAGE:

A)Paying cash for his Mercedes.

B)Buying an extravagant fur for his wife.

C)His closet full of expensive suits, shoes and clothes.

D)Smiling at the cute bank teller as he handed her another easily earned deposit of cash.

BACK TO SCENE

MC walked out of the bathroom. His pager vibrated as he entered the reception area and started the coffee. He looked at the number shown on the pager.

MC leaned into the marble trim on the window, gazing at the fog rolling in over the lake. The sound of the brewing coffee shared his company.

>			TINA
> Smells good. Is it that the imported stuff?

MC doesn't respond. The receptionist, TINA, who is MC's sister-in-law, startled him as she walked through the mirrored glass doors. She tossed the morning dailies, on her desk. MC picked one of them up and unrolled it.

        TINA
Someone called yesterday. I left the messages on your desk by the phone. Did you get them?

Two of Lois' articles are on the front page. MC looked closer at the byline.

INSERT NEWSPAPER ARTICLE:

by Lois DuSol

Still no arrest, police stall case

BACK TO SCENE

        MC
Yeah. Oh, and I need copies of the Harmon brief and please make me an appointment with the Ledger Company's chairman before I leave for court today.

        MC
How's my wife doing these days?

        TINA
She's doing okay. I don't get to see much of her. You know she's opening a new clinic over in the old neighborhood. She found a new partner too. He has a good reputation. And he's a gentleman.

        MC
Yeah, she mentioned something like that the last time we spoke.

        TINA
When was that, MC?

MC didn't reply but instead, disappeared into his office, grabbed his briefcase and walked out of the office, taking the newspaper with him.

        MC
I'll be out of the office today. Page me if anyone

important calls.

MC waited until he was outside of the building to return the page.

          MC
Yes, I got a page.

          SLICK
We should meet up sometime today to discuss our new arrangement but in the meanwhile you should head on over to the Hotel by the airport, we have a few guests over there waiting.

          MC
Okay. How about six, I'll meet you over at your place. In the meanwhile, I'll call a few friends of my own. I get half.

          SLICK
Okay, half--on everything. No excuses.

          MC
Come on man, I do work, you know.

MC puts away his phone and heads toward his car, smiling. Once inside his car he calls his friend, who known to everyone as HOODLUM.

          MC
Good morning. Your presence is requested by a few beautiful women at the hotel airport--usual cut for me.

          HOODLUM
I'm on my way.

Smiling a little, MC hangs up the phone and places it inside the glove box as a snapshot of his wife and children tumbles onto the passenger seat. MC looks at the picture and placed it back inside, shutting it soundly.

INT: NEWSROOM-SIX MONTHS LATER-DAY

Lois, now, no longer pregnant, is on the phone with the police. She is at a computer furiously typing and summoning her editor, FRANK PERSONS. Frank approaches Lois' desk and stands there with his hands on his hips.

          LOIS

Ok, here is the scoop. Police are still looking for
the murderer of Toyman and they want the media to
help by running an artist's sketch of the suspects.

Frank just looks at Lois with no response. She's trying to hand him a press release about it.

          LOIS
They're sending a photo of the car they were last
seen in and a description of one of them.

          FRANK
Anything else?

          LOIS
No.

          FRANK
They had two men in custody six months ago but they
let them go and instead, questioned two kids and
then let them go. I wonder why...

          FRANK
Think Lois. Use your head.

Lois sits at her desk. She picks up the phone again.

          LOIS
Yes, may I speak to Sgt. Pete again?

Lois starts to write hurriedly in her notebook and soon hangs up. She walks toward the Frank's office.

          LOIS
How did you know they were going to arrest the boys
this time? They've been in and out of there for half
the year? We ran a story accusing them of stalling
the case!

          FRANK
I didn't know, Lois, but you gotta ask the right
questions. Be direct.

          LOIS
I was.

FRANK
Besides, I hear things. And one of the detectives working on the case is an old drinking buddy of mine from back in the day. He told me the two adult male suspects they questioned on the scene told them they saw two kids hanging around in the area where the body was found a day or so before they found him.

LOIS
Yeah, but they're only seven and eight. Kids that young don't kill. This whole thing is strange. How is it that you can question suspects over and over again for eight months? That cannot be legal.

FRANK
They got arrested, okay. Don't go over the edge on this one. We're not mercenaries.

LOIS
They released a statement that they had been looking for two adult males with a history of violent crimes and drug activity. Then they questioned two little kids--on the advisement of two adult males with a history of narcotics and violence. It's hard to believe they would take their information seriously. They'd do anything to stay out of prison.

FRANK
Listen, they may or may not charge the kids--they can hold them for three days after the arrest. They keep coming back to these boys and they are the only ones who have been arrested. I was told they are planning to hold a press conference today. Now either they'll get the boys charged today or they'll cancel the press conference--and that'll be the end of this. But they already got a confession out of them last night. They plan to have a press conference this evening. Experience tells me if they get the witnesses, they're going to charge those boys. Now that's a story.

Frank turns and starts to walk away as he shouts instructions to Lois over his shoulder.

FRANK
Lois, write up what you have and make sure you're at

that press conference. Oh, by the way--why don't you
ask the cops why so many interviews.

          LOIS
Okay. They're also having a rally for the boys. One
of the boys' mother wants to make a televised appeal
for help to get a lawyer.

          FRANK
Well, it looks like you're going to be busy today.
Try to remember to get some lunch.

Lois nods in agreement and leaves the office.

INT: G-MAN'S OFFICE-SECLUDED WAREHOUSE-DAY

A local crime boss, GERALD MANNING, is holding a gun on the two men who told police they saw the two boys commit the murder of Toyman. Gerald is known to his colleagues as G-MAN.

He shoots around both men who are tied to a metal pole near the ceiling. Their feet dance in the air as they twist their bodies trying to avoid being shot.

          G-MAN
Who told you to kill Toyman? Who are you two working
for?

         THUG 1
Man, I told you, I ain't working for nobody.

Gangster turns to Thug 2 and points the gun at him.

          G-MAN
Who are you working for?

         THUG 2
I don't want to die, man we just needed the money.
They said all we had to do was be there when the
police showed up and say we saw the kids do it. I
didn't know it would turn out like this.

Thug 1 turns his head in disgust, mumbling.

          G-MAN
Oh, so you didn't think the police would believe you

or you didn't think they would arrest the boys?

The men just dangle from their arms not saying anything.

> G-MAN
> Do you know who killed Toyman?

> G-MAN
> So, you don't know who killed Toyman.

The men quickly shake their heads.

> G-MAN
> Nobody will be able to find you here because I got a
> bad memory too.

G-Man puts away his gun and walks out of the warehouse leaving the men dangling from the plumbing.

INT: MC'S CONDO-BEDROOM-DAY

MC sits shirtless on the side of his round bed. He looks at a Palm Pilot, checking appointments and then pads through a thick shag to his laptop, putting the finishing touches on a brief.

His soothing alarm pops on for the third time and the clock reads a blurry 4:30 a.m. until he reaches for his glasses. He puts on his watch and reaches for the phone, returning calls from his pager. One of those calls is to his mother.

> MC
> Ma, it's me. Call me back.

INT: MC'S CAR

MC, stuffing a muffin into his mouth, rolls out of his garage in his most prized possession--a convertible Mercedes, silver in color and loaded with status. MC takes a deep lung full of morning air. He puts the top down, then the phone rings. It's his mother.

INTERCUT PHONE CONVERSATION:

> MC:
> Hello?

INT. MA'S KITCHEN-DAY

There is a bustle of excitement swirling around Ma, catching her attention every now and again. She nervously switches the phone from ear to ear.

  MA:
MC, the police just arrested the boys.

  MC,
What boys, ma?

  MA:
The two little boys on the news. The ones they're trying to say killed Toyman. Wilma and the one boy's mother is over here now. How soon can you get here?

  MC
I thought they already had a lawyer?

  MA
They did but she asked to be removed from the case.

  MC
I'm on my way to court Ma. I can't take on any more free battles again. Do they have any money. Maybe I can make a referral...

  MA
Make a what? After all we have done for you?

  Mc
Like what ma?

  MA:
Like feed you when you were starving to death trying to get through school. Remember all those trips up there--with care baskets in tow? I wasn't the only one helping you, baby. We all helped here in the community.

  MC:
I know Ma. I know, but I still have to eat. I did the last case pro bono and got Willa Mae's boy out of that trouble--I could go on but my debt is paid, let me set the record straight. My debt is paid, Ma.

MA
The debt is never paid boy. Don't start with me.
Wilma and Gina look up to you and those boys need
your help. all of these people look up to you around
here.

MC
You can't keep using me as your social outlet and
community avenger. I cannot be everyone's hero.

MA
You don't have to be a hero--anymore. And I don't
use anyone...you just want me to beg you to do this

MC:
Yes, you do. Remember our discussion last week. No
more volunteer services. That means no fundraiser,
lost causes or anything, ok?

A sudden roar in the background breaks Ma's concentration and she turns
around. A news telecast can be heard in the background and people are
walking back and forth, all around Ma.

MA:
Ok, but what do I tell these people.

MC
What people. I thought it was Gina and Wilma.

MA:
Well, son, you know the neighborhood is all stirred
up about this killing and why the investigation took
so long to complete and then the arrest of the boys.
They've kind of gathered here as a base of operations
and...

MC:
Base of operations? Ma, say to me that you are not
involved in something controversial. I thought you
disbanded that block club you started. How many
people are at the house?

MA:
Oh, your sister counted 300 but that was at 7:00
a.m. so, you get the picture, I think CNN and FOX is
here too, I'm not sure but they told me they were

17

coming but...

Mc is quiet and has let bits of muffin fall around his Armani suit and Versace tie ensemble. He stops short almost going through a red light.

    MC
CNN. CNN is at the house--this is the very last time Ma. You cannot be a heroine to everybody. Where's Dad, how's he holding up--never mind, don't answer that. I'll let him tell me what's going on when I get there. Ma, I'm on my way to court so I should be there about noon or so, ok?

    MA
Ok Mc. You're still my sweet little man after all these years... bring some paper plates and silverware..

Mc holds the cell away from his ear, silently laughing.

    MC
Bye Ma.

Mc hangs up shaking his head. Calls second chair

INT. SYDNEY'S-BEDROOM-DAY

SYDNEY is sitting upright in bed with his wife, who is now rolling away from him.

    SYDNEY
Hello?

    SYDNEY'S WIFE
Who is that?

    SYDNEY
MC. I'll be brief, hon.

    MC:
It's me. Sorry to wake you but just listen. You know they put those boys in jail. I grew up with the one little boy's momma and the other one's parents have the retainer, so I'm thinking about taking them both...

MC hesitates.

>   MC
> ...Although, I'd rather have some help on this one.
> Third chair said he'll be there but you know I want
> you in on this one. We can win this, easily. You
> know they didn't do it..."

SECOND CHAIR'S BEDROOM

Mc's voice trailed off because Second wasn't listening anymore. He sighs an old man's sigh into the phone. He inches himself down into the bed, under the blankets before answering him.

>   SYDNEY
> O.K. Call me after court.

Second chair hung up and drifted back to sleep.

>   SYDNEY'S WIFE
> Don't tell me Martin is considering taking that
> heater case, Sydney.

>   SYDNEY'S WIFE
> There is something strange about that case--that's
> why I dropped it.

>   SYDNEY'S WIFE
> You know, you're not the only one in this house who
> practices law. When are you going to tell him--
> dissolve the partnership? We can make more money
> defending drug dealers and greedy husbands. Why
> this, still? What are you trying to prove and who
> are you trying to be--Medger Evers?

>   SYDNEY
> What do you want me to say? I don't know what to say
> to you, now or to him later on today. Stop nagging
> me. I will tell him about our plans but not now,

>   SYDNEY'S WIFE
> Why is it he always seems to get more of a
> percentage on the cases? Isn't that enough reason to
> quit?

>   SYDNEY

. I said leave it alone. Go back to sleep.

INT: MC CAR-DAY

MC makes another call. He phones Hoodlum.

          HOODLUM
Hello.

          MC
Go to the airport Hotel tonight, wait inside the bar and bring your buddy. There will be two of them there.

          HOODLUM
OK.

EXT. TOWN COURTHOUSE-DAY

MC runs into Lois. Since she has been covering police and courts for her newspaper, they have become friendly. She is covering many of the crime stories about Toyman's murder and some of MC's other cases.

          MC
Lois, what are you doing here?

          LOIS
I work here, remember? What's up.

          MC
I have two new clients, little boys.

Mc looks into her brown eyes.

          LOIS
Oh, you mean from the story I broke last week? It's good someone in this town still has some integrity-- good luck with it. You're finally in your league.

          MC
Whatever. You know--you sure have gotten cocky lately.

Lois smiles and turns around, tossing her hair, switching away. Mc watches her as she walks up to two assistant states attorneys and walks her walk down the hall, trailing them. He goes inside one of the courtrooms.

INT. COURTROOM HALLWAY

When Mc walked out of the courtroom he sees Lois, alone in the courthouse hallway, sitting on a bench writing. He approaches.

        MC
Lois.

Startled, she looks up. Then she stands up and walks toward him.

        LOIS
Yes, sir, how can I help you?

        MC
You know about the rally, right?

        LOIS
Yeah, I knew but thanks for telling me. I'll see ya there.

Lois awkwardly fumbles in her bag. Mc hesitates, noticing her flashy new look.

        MC
You look nice-er

        LOIS
Thanks. You do too--except for this.

Lois softly brushes imaginary crumbs off of his mustache, touching the side of his mouth,

        LOIS
You smell good too.

She then walks away.

EXT: MA'S HOUSE

There is a huge crowd spilling from Ma's front yard into the street and all over the small block. Mc is astonished at the amount of support the two children have. Mc's mother is standing on the porch talking to a television producer.

        MA

Here he comes.

The crowd of people part to let him through and start an enormous cheer for MC.

HERRA a vain, out-of-work actress who is dating MC, is also in the crowd. She pushes her way to the front, grabbing him by the arm. He turns around and happily kisses her.

          MC
When'd you get into town?

          HERRA
I jumped on a flight as soon as I heard--baby you
are the talk of the nation!

          MC
This is national already huh?

Herra squeezes his butt, kisses him, and shoos him toward his mother. Ma sees the exchange and looks miffed.

          MA
And who is that? Aren't you still married.

          MC
Ma, not now, don't you have enough going on? Besides
Christine and the kids are okay. They live right
across the street from me. I see the kids every day.
It's almost as if she didn't go anywhere.

          MA
She's smart. I always told you she was a smart girl.
She's not letting you get too far away.

          MC
Yeah, yeah Ma. Who are all of these people and where
is my father?

MC's father is sitting in a lawn chair in the back yard, reading a newspaper, shielded from all of the fanfare. He waves at his son and MC waves back.

          MA
The CNN and Fox television producers would like to
talk to you about the segment.

                    MC
          Segment. Ma, you know about segments now? Where is
          the producer.

                    MA
          Over there. Go ahead baby, shine!

Ma's friends gather around Ma beaming right along with her. Mc smiles awkwardly.

                    MC
          Maybe it's a better idea if you first point out
          Wilma and Gina. Where are they?

                    MA
          In the house sweetie, sitting around the kitchen
          table.

Mc hands his mother a bag with the paper supplies she asked for and enters the home.

INT. MA'S KITCHEN

Two women are seated inside a darkened kitchen at a table with a bottle of wine between them.

The women, Wilma and Gina have swollen eyes and untouched glasses of wine.

                    MC
          Good afternoon ladies, my name is Martin Combs, but
          you can call me MC. I'm going to get the police to
          release your babies from jail.

Series of Shots:

A) The women introduce themselves as the aunts of the boys.

B) The women hand over assorted documents and photographs.

C) MC pulls out contracts for the women to sign.

D) Gina removes from her lap a large envelope of money and hands it to MC.

Back to scene

                    WILMA
          MC, my nephew is a son to me. He is a baby. Get him
          out of there please. I mean--what can I do to make
          them realize that no child can commit the type of
          crime they arrested him for? No child.

                    GINA
          Look, that's nine thousand dollars. I don't know
          what your retainer is but I hope this is enough.
          We're serious. I want you to not only get my baby
          outta jail but prosecute the bastards who arrested
          him in the first place. I'm suing this town. I'm
          sick of their racist practices.

Gina stands up, running her fingers through her now perfectly coifed and longer hair. She picks up a glass of wine from the table.

                    GINA
          When I saw them let those thugs go free and come
          after my son...

Gina slumps down in a chair, holding the glass of wine in one hand and her head in another.

MC raises his eyebrows as he looks inside the envelope.

                    GINA
          I hope it's enough. It's all we have.

MC sat down with the women, grabbing their hands. He lowers his head in prayer. Gina put down the glass of wine.

                    MC
          Let us pray.

Mc leads the women in silent prayer They end the prayer.

                    MC
          We're gonna need all the help we can get, ladies.
          Let's go meet the press.

MC leads Gina and Wilma by the hand out of the kitchen.

EXT. MA'S HOUSE

The crowd has grown larger by the time MC and the women emerge from the house. Police have begun to show up, surrounding the crowd.

Mc uses his mother's porch as a platform as the cameras begin to roll.

Lois drives up to the rally, jumping out of her car in time to catch the event.

>   MC
> Good afternoon everyone. Many of you know who I am
> and for those of you who don't, I am the man
> representing those two little boys' police arrested
> and threw in jail this morning. I am the man who
> will free the children. And as I understand, the
> boys have not been charged so I expect them home
> soon.

Applause from the crowd.

>   MC
> These women, Gina and Wilma are the relatives of the
> two boys' police ripped from their beds in the middle
> of the night. They will need the support of the
> community. Thank you and the boys thank you.

MC raises his arms, still holding on to the women. The crowd roars and chant "Free our boys."

INT. POLICE HEADQUARTERS-DAY

Across town, at the city's police headquarters, there was another kind of meeting taking place.

Eighteen months ago, A federal agent with a newly formed CIA-FBI task force was sent from Washington D.C. to the city to investigate allegations of public corruption.

CHARLEY HUFF is nearing retirement and wants to go out on a high note but after year in the town, he has only passed on low-level federal busts. He wants to be the man who cleaned up the town but because of his age, temperament, and the level of corruption, he can't get a break on the big bust. He is meeting with one of his contacts, Farley Douglas, who is a top public official in the small city.

Douglas, a career politician, knows how to play ball with the best of them because in his mind a payoff is just a tip. TUNKS is an ex-cop who took a civilian job with the force just for the pay and to be near the action. He breaks into their private meeting.

> TUNKS
> Hey Farley, can I talk to you a minute?

Farley gets up and leaves the room.

INT: HALLWAY

> TUNKS
> Here's the paper work on the Fenwick case.

Farley reads the through the file and starts to scribble his signature

> FARLEY
> Who made the arrest? Crowe and Marrsec?

> TUNKS
> Yeah, but what does it matter now? The boys are arrested and now they're charged.

Tunks takes the file and starts to walk away. Farley stops him.

> FARLEY
> My God, I hope you realize that these two kids aren't getting out of jail.

> TUNKS
> Look at it this way: Our officers have arrested the youngest murders in the nation. Who would have ever figured an five and six year old could pull off the hit of the year?

Farley dabs at his forehead with a handkerchief.

> FARLEY
> We don't have the option of hoping no one contests this arrest and we go on with our lives. I've got to go and explain to that fucking federal agent and Mr. and Mrs. Public how you had to get some thugs to kill a local toy store owner for laundering money for some punk you couldn't arrest when you were on the force.

Charley enters the hallway.

> CHARLEY
> Excuse me gentlemen. Farley, we can pick this up another time.

> FARLEY
> No, it's just that we have this case we need to rap up--you know, the kids who got arrested this morning.

> CHARLEY
> Yeah, I read something about that. Any charges yet.

> FARLEY
> No, not yet. Hey, why don't we meet later--I'll get us lunch.

> CHARLEY
> Look, if you guys need me to send the taskforce down to help get this cleaned up...

> FARLEY
> No, uh no--it's fine. We're okay here.

Charley put on his hat and walked away. The men entered the office.

The Charley and Farley look at each other.

> TUNKS
> So, how's it gonna be, Boss?

Farley walks over to his desk and punches the intercom button on the phone.

> FARLEY
> Call the chief. Tell him to go ahead with the announcement of charges.

> TUNKS
> If this works, we may have a new way of doing things.

> FARLEY
> Hell, the public wanted the case solved--now it's solved. This is extra, Tunks, I mean it. You need to start making this more worth my while.

> TUNKS
> Sure. Good choice, Boss. Oh, by the way--how's the yacht?

Tunks slaps Farley on the back and walks out of the room.

EXT. MA'S HOUSE-DAY

Lois stands among the crowd taking notes and interviewing people. She answers her cell phone and begins to cut through the crowd. After pushing her way to the front of the crowd, she encounters Herra. She taps MC on the shoulder.

> LOIS
> Mc, Mc they've charged the boys. Police brought charges against the boys. I gotta go but let me get a response from you now.

Mc turns around to see both Lois and Herra standing in front of him. Lois shoved her tape recorder in his face. Then turns to Herra.

> LOIS
> Hi, I'm Lois. Are you MC's new secretary?

> HERRA
> Lois? I guess that would make you Superman.

Herra glares at MC. And places her sunglasses on her eyes.

> MC
> No. This is Lois DuSol. I'll be right back.

> MC

Lois, how do you know this?

> LOIS
> My editor just called me. Police are having a press conference in a half-hour. I gotta go--Superman.

Lois snickered and watched as Mc walked towards Herra. He whispers in Herra's ear and she nods in agreement then walks towards her car. MC returns to the porch to tell Gina and Wilma the news. The women sob and return to the kitchen.

> MC

Ma, how are you going to disperse these people from
your yard? I'm leaving in a few, I have to prepare
and meet with my clients.

     MA

You don't worry about me, go ahead and do what you
have to. When the food runs out, they'll leave.

     MC

That's another thing. Where did you all get the
money for all of this? There has to be at least a
thousand people out here.

     MA

It's funny you should ask because Gina and Wilma
arranged for all of this. You know Gina has had her
problems but I've never seen her like this. I don't
know where she's getting all of this money.

     MC

I'm heading down to the police station, Ma, I'll
call you later and fill you in.

As the crowd began to disperse, G-man, there among the crowd of people, smoking a cigar and staring in MC's direction. He turns and jumps into an expensive SUV and zooms off.

INT. G-MAN'S SUV-DAY

G-man is sitting in his truck watching Wilma, Gina, Herra and MC as they get ready to go to the police station. He also spots Lois in the crowd.

     G-MAN

Hello? Wilma, did you tell MC what I told you to
tell him?

     WILMA

Yes, I did, G. Thank you for this. We don't know
what we would have done without your help. The boys
are charged now so we have to go by the police
station to here what they have to say.

     G-MAN

I heard. Don't worry, He'll get them out. I'll make
sure of it. Besides, he looks pretty honest. Did you
see Her standing out there?

                    WILMA
          Yeah, that was strange. I wonder how they met?

                    G-MAN
          I wonder too. Tell Gina to fix herself up a little--
          she looked high on national television. You know I
          hate to see that.

                    WILMA
          G, you know that woman hasn't been the same since
          you left, so don't expect too much. I'm going to
          visit Tony's mother's grave later today. He had been
          asking about doing that before all of this happened.
          He's been through so much.

                    G-MAN
          Let Gina know I'll be by to see her later on
          tonight. I really don't want to talk about Tony's
          mother right now, Wilma. She was an addict. Tony
          doesn't need that in his life. He's got enough
          problems.

G-Man puts away the cell phone.

EXT: MA'S HOUSE

Mc walks away from his mother, waving a silent good bye. He walked quickly to his car. He motions for Gina and Wilma to join him.

INT:BOARD ROOM WASHINGTON D.C.-DAY

Seven men are seated around a conference table listening to Charley via speakerphone. An older man, Lawrence Slattery, sits at the head of the table.

                    CHARLEY
          It's about to hit the fan up here. I guess you can
          gather that from my report. What's our next move?

                    SLATTERY
          Well, you can start planning your retirement
          destination, Charley because thanks to your
          information we can arrest anyone of those crooks and
          get to who is behind all of that dirty money.

CHARLEY
As I stated in my report, it's going to be tough to prove in court. They're aren't many willing to break the silence.

SLATTERY
By your estimates, there's at least 86 billion in dirty money being brought through there on a weekly basis. They aren't alone up there. Someone is at the top.

SLATTERY
See if you can find someone who isn't in with them. I know it's hard but we've only got a little less than week to prove ourselves down here. We have to make a significant dent in their armor--quickly. Get you wiretap list in order.

CHARLEY
I'm on it. I'll report back at the end of the week.

The call is disconnected. Charley sitting in his car, outside of Lois' newsroom. There is a copy of the newspaper with her article in the passenger seat. He starts the car and drives away.

EXT. SLICK'S MIRAGE-DAY

Gangster, puffing a Cuban cigar and keeping time to loud Hip Hop music, speeds down the street. He stops his SUV at a popular nightclub owned by his boyhood friend, SLICK.

INT. SLICK'S MIRAGE

Inside of the empty, mirrored club, a jukebox is spilling smooth jazz tunes through it's speakers.

G-Man enters and the bartender picks up the phone and talks. After a few seconds Slick, walks toward Gangster. They sit down and the bartender pours them each a shot.

G-MAN
I'm sorry about Toyman. I didn't know they would do that. He was my friend too.

SLICK
Never underestimate. This town belongs to them, I

told you that before all this shit went down. Now
they got three of your people: The boys and Toyman.
You ain't gone have nobody left. Leave it alone.

        G-MAN

Leave what alone. They fuckin' with me. They're
doing the same thing I'm doing but on a much larger
scale and with more people. What kind of threat
could I have been?

        SLICK,

It don't matter. Look, find another line of work
before you get killed. I can't help you.

        G-MAN

I can't. I have to find someone else to replace
Toyman. And you are the replacement so don't refuse.
I know Toyman was your friend. He and I had many
discussions about you and yawls plans for
retirement. Now he's retired. So unless you're
looking to retire right now, I suggest you
cooperate.

        SLICK,

You're crazy. Why me?

        G-MAN

You're the only business I can fuck with right now--
that can handle large amounts of money. And I don't
give a fuck about you--just like Toyman. But see
that's my whole problem in a nutshell. Everybody I
know is a small-time punk. but For now, that's all I
have. My little cousins are in jail for a murder
they didn't commit and the same greedy asses who
arrested them killed Toyman--all to get a little
piece of the action. And they'll kill you too. The
only thing keeping you alive is all of the publicity
the arrest caused. You can thank all those nosy ass
reporters for that shit.

        SLICK

Oh, I see. We're all going to die. Okay. What makes
you think you can come up in here--by yourself--and
talk this shit.

        G-MAN

Do you like owning this bar?

        SLICK
Yeah.

        G-MAN
All your permits in order?

        SLICK
What?

        G-MAN
I know you don't think that much about me but this is what I do. I got enough connections, just one or two filthy politicians in my pocket, to shut this juke joint down. So play or go home. Or disappear-- you got life insurance? Hate to see that stripper you just married go hungry.

Gangster stops his tirade for a second. Walks around swinging his arms. He drops a few coins in the juke box and dances with an imaginary partner. Helper sits at the table, glaring at the lanky man spin and twist.

        SLICK
Why you in here fuckin' with me, G-man? We grew up together--we're boys.

Gangster stops his dance, and lets out a sigh. He starts to walk towards Slick.

        G-MAN
I can count on you, can't I, Slick?

        SLICK
Yeah, man. I ain't got no real choice, do I.

        G-MAN
No. Back-in-the-day boys do this kind of thing for each other, don't they?

Gangster starts to walk away. The soulful music continues to blare angrily as Gangster leaves. He stops to say one more thing.

        G-MAN
Maybe you do have a choice. Better hope Mc gets those boys outta trouble and this weight off of my

back. And the longer that takes, the better off we'll be--you're not exactly wealthy, are you?

Slick just sits there.

          G-MAN
I'll send somebody to see you.

EXT. SLICK'S MIRAGE-NIGHT

G-Man leaves the club and gets back into his SUV and drives off. Nearby, Tunks is sitting in his car photographing him. He calls Crowe, who arrested the boys.

          CROWE
Yeah, who is it.

          TUNKS
I have G-man in my line of fire. He's over here at Slick's but I don't know what the hell they talked about because that new mike you planted ain't worth a damn. I couldn't hear a thing. Where's Herra.

          CROWE
She's over at MC's office. They haven't even done it yet. We got a tail on Lois. She's is out with her co-workers at the pub. You never would figure her for a drinker. It was hard as hell getting Mc's condo and office wired up.

          TUNKS
Who did it?

          CROWE
Sal. I got him to light up the whole floor. MC can't go anywhere without me seeing it. Sal went over to his condo and did some free electrical work on his honor's Jacuzzi last week. He's got a lot of nerve taking that punk's case.

          TUNKS
Why not. Everyone's always writing about his cases especially Lois. You ought to hear her on the phone, weaseling information out of people. She used to call me all of the time--until, well you know. Hell, when I found out I wasn't getting a pension, I

told her whatever I knew. Fuck 'em. I won't making
enough to live on anyways.

          CROWE
Yeah, I know. People like G-Man get all the money.

          TUNKS
I finally got G-Man in a corner. I could never catch
him with anything--nothing stuck. I'm glad things
worked out the way they did because I'm retiring
after this. It's no kind of a life for me. I got
nothing now, because one of his punk flunkies
complained about an arrest. The piece of shit raped
a kid and I kicked his ass. What thanks do I get?

          TUNKS
I don't understand it. We bust our asses and we get
nothing. Except a bullet to the chest. We gotta do
this right, Tunks. We gotta get that money.

          TUNKS
 Yeah, he's bringing in too much dough around here
to not know how to share.

          TUNKS
Lois is a good kid but she's pissin' on some of the
top dogs around here. Who knows, I might can
blackmail someone with the stuff she digs up.

          CROWE
Yeah, I see. We got wires everywhere. If they get
brave we can get them without it getting messy.
Blackmail is a wonderful thing.

Both men hang-up. Tunks drives off following G-Man while Crowe returns to
watching Mc and Herra on the hidden camera/closed circuit tv. Sal
installed. He sees the pair turn off the light to the office.

EXT. PUB

G-Man stops by a local Pub for a beer and to think. Lois is there with her
co-workers. When he enters he sees them and sits at the bar. Lois gets up
to get another drink and Gangster strikes up a conversation with her. Tunks
is outside of the establishment, waiting.

          G-MAN

Hey, aren't you the one who wrote about those boys being arrested.

        LOIS,
Yes, How did you know it was me?

        G-MAN
I guessed. Sit with me a while--your friends won't mind, will they?

Lois shakes her head no and sits down. They talk, laugh and take sips of their drink. G-Man hands Lois his business card. It says: Gerald Manning, Private Detective.

        LOIS
I guess this is where you get the nickname G-Man.

Lois places the card in her purse.

G-Man shrugs his shoulders and caresses Lois' hand. Then he looks at Lois intently and motions to pay for her drink. Lois declines.

        LOIS
I should be getting back to my friends. I guess we'll see each other around.

        G-MAN
We will.

Lois sashays back to her table touching her hair, making sure it's still in place. Her friends saw the exchange between the two.

        LOIS
He is so fine, damn. I never thought I'd find anyone that suave in this town.

        CO-WORKER 1
Ohhh, what happened to MC? I thought he was the finest man alive.

        CO-WORKER 2
Shit, he looks just like him. Tall, suave, handsome. At least you got good taste girl. I hope you didn't give him your number. We don't need another stalker, do we?

LOIS
No, we don't need a another stalker but I will never mind a fine ass brother like that holding on to me. I told him we'd meet again. He said he saw me at the rally. He's new in town and just opened an office on Main St. He's interested in the case too.

CO-WORKER 2
Why? Don't tell me he's a lawyer too.

LOIS
Nope. He's a private detective. See, here is his card.

CO-WORKER 1
You're insane girl.

CO-WORKER 2
I guess you still don't know where your husband is, as small as this place is.

LOIS
No, and thanks for the bring-down. Girl, these bucks running around here ain't thinking about me and mine. They're just out, like any other man, kickin' it. Even MC. So what can I do about someone else's activities? Hmm? Anyone?

CO-WORKER 2
Nothin'.

The women give Lois' tirade a moment of silence while they sip on their drinks.

LOIS
I guess his triflin' ass will pop up when he gets tired of running around in the streets.

CO-WORKER 1
Will you take him back?

LOIS
Probably. It's a shame ain't it?

CO-WORKER 1
Yeah, girl it is a shame.

                    LOIS
          It's a shame you ain't gotta man to look for.

                    CO-WORKER 1
          I heard that.

G-man watch as the women giggle and sneak looks in his direction. He orders something to eat then moves to another location in the pub. He sits away from bar so that he can get a better view of Lois as they leave the Pub.

INT: TUNKS' CAR

Tunks snaps photographs of Lois as she strolls out of the pub with her friends.

TUNK'S FLASHBACK: EXT: A HIGHWAY SHOULDER-DAY

A younger G-MAN is speeding along the highway playing loud music and puffing furiously on a Cuban cigar. His SUV is soon pulled over in traffic by a patrolman. The officer, a younger Tunks, gets out of his squad car and approaches the flashy truck.

                    G-MAN
          Yes, officer, may I help you?

G-Man starts to pull out his registration and license. He looks over at the officer as he hands the items to him.

                    TUNKS
          I don't need to see those. I know who you are. Now
          step out of the vehicle.

G-man gets out of the truck slowly, taking his cigar with him. Crowe leads him to the squad car and the men get inside.

                    TUNKS
          Everyone knows who you are and everyone knows what
          you do but what perplexes me is that you don't
          answer to anyone. Who in the fuck do you think you
          are?

                    G-MAN
          A man. Look you want a bribe or something? Maybe I
          can arrange for a little drop off...

> TUNKS
> 50-50 or you go out of business today.

G-Man puffed on his cigar. Then he got out of the squad car, slamming the door behind him.

> G-MAN
> If you approach me again, you will regret it. You have a good day.

Tunks pulls out his handcuffs and gets out of the squad car. He grabs G-man by the back of his collar, spins him around shoves him against the hood of the SUV, attempting to place the cuffs on.

But G-man squirms out of his grasp and head butts the officer, taking his revolver before he hits the ground. Tunks pulls another weapon from an ankle holster and fires a shot at G-man as he leaps behind the wheel of his truck and speeds away. Turning to get up off of the ground, Tunks sees a burning cigar on the ground, dropped in the scuffle by G-Man. He gets up and drives off in his squad car. His cell phone rings.

> TUNKS
> Yeah, who is it?

> CROWE
> Hey, it's me. I think I still need some help on this Sergeant's exam, it's pretty tough.

> TUNKS
> Yeah, I'll be in the station about 4 p.m. We can go over some things then.

Tunks puts away the cell phone.

FLASHBACK CON'T-ONE YEAR LATER-INT: POLICE AUDITORIUM

Tunks stands before a committee of police commissioners who sit on a local governing board. He is looking at a thick packet of information listing the charges against him.

The words say: conduct unbecoming of an officer and assault and battery. It lists several incidents where he has brutalized people during the course of his career.

The bundle of papers quivers in his sweaty hands. The sparse gathering in the huge auditorium responded in a weak applause for the actions of the board.

> COMMISSIONER
> Sgt. Oliver Tunks, the board has moved to relieve you of all duties.

G-Man sits in the back of the auditorium unnoticed at the public hearing. He is dressed conservatively in a dark suit and is holding a briefcase. He leaves as quietly as he had entered.

END FLASHBACK

INT: TUNK'S CAR-PRESENT DAY

Tunks takes a quick swig of whiskey and gets out of his car. He opens the trunk and pumps .12 gauge shotguns, taking aim it at G-Man's SUV.

The pellets ignite the gas tank and the explosion shatters the glass windows at the Pub. Patrons scream, run out of the establishment and scramble for cover as Tunks hops into his car and drives away.

G-Man stumbles out of the pub. He calmly walks away from the excitement and makes a call. In about five minutes, a man pulls up and G-Man gets into his truck. They drive away.

INT: LOIS' CAR

Nearly a mile away, Lois hears the explosion and then turns on a news radio station. Impatiently, she calls police dispatch.

> POLICE DISPATCHER
> Dispatcher.

> LOIS
> Just doing a beat check. Anything unusual tonight?

> POLICE DISPATCHER
> Lois?

> LOIS
> Yeah.

> POLICE DISPATCHER
> Oh--I'm not used to you working nights. Yeah, we just got a call of a fire over there by the pub. There may have been an explosion.

LOIS
Okay, thanks.

Lois turns her car around and heads towards the pandemonium outside of the pub.

EXT. MC'S HOT TUB-NIGHT

Mc and Herra share his new hot tub and a bottle of chilled champagne.

MC
I'd like to thank you for helping me out. It's been working out fine so far. Except for my wife moving out and all. For the first time in my life I've actually felt lonely.

Herra eases over to Mc and gently gives him a back rub.

HERRA
It's been hard for me too. I still don't know what to do with myself. There isn't anything out there for me now. I remember when I had to turn offers down. What happens when the curtain closes?

Herra reaches over Mc for her glass of champagne.

HERRA
Did those dates work out for you? I mean did the women enjoy themselves?

MC
Yeah, actually I did too. It helps having something like that to do after work. I don't even mind that they're old. I mean one woman--she was loaded, She had to be about 70. I was looking for her to slip out of pair of sexy Depends.

HERRA
You're a trip, Mc. The objective is to keep 'em happy, not sleep with them.

MC
Hold on now. Sometimes they want something extra, if you know what I mean. A lot of extra. She kept touching me.

Herra starts giggling and eventually they begin to kiss. they have sex in the hot tub.

INT: MC'S BEDROOM-NIGHT

Mc rolls over searching for Herra's warmth but she's not there. MC's pager wakes him up soon after. He noticed that Herra left while he was sleeping again. He looks at the pager, scrolling through old e-mail messages and finds a new one from Hoodlum. MC picks up the phone.

          MC
What's going on?

          HOODLUM
I need some more buddies.

          MC
How many?

          HOODLUM
Three more. They want to party.

          MC
I'll call Slick

Mc hangs up the phone and calls his buddy Slick.

Slick is riding in his car when the phone rings.

          SLICK
Hello.

          MC
We need three more for tonight. Who can you find?

          SLICK
You mean I need two more outside of yourself.

          MC
I'm tired. Not tonight.

          SLICK
Make it your business to be there. That's why you get paid as much as you do.

> SLICK
> I'll be there with two of my friends.

MC hung up the phone, got out of bed and starts to get dressed. He looked at the clock. It reads 1:30 a.m. He hopped in his car and sped towards the Hotel near the airport.

NEXT DAY-EXT. COURTHOUSE-DAY-PROBABLE CAUSE HEARING

A bunch of nosy, self-righteous, citizens picketers surrounded MC when he entered the courthouse. They blamed MC for stirring up trouble for all of the working class in the neighborhood. .

> GROUP MEMBER
> Why don't you let this go? How do you know those
> little hoods aren't guilty. I'm tired of the police
> hassling me and my family every time we leave our
> house. YOU DON'T EVEN LIVE OVER THERE ANYMORE.

> MC
> You have more guilt than they do, They're innocent
> children. What are you? You reminds me of the whore
> that sat at the temple door. The only difference
> between you and another streetwalker is that the
> government allows you to flourish. If they were to
> take away the crumbs they've allowed you to have,
> you would die in an instant.

The other members of the group drew back in a collective gasp. He walked proudly towards the courtroom.

INT. COURTROOM--PROBABLE CAUSE HEARING

The sound of rustling paper fills the courtroom along with a hushed murmur. As MC approached, Sydney and another lawyer interested in the case, watched the expressions of the audience in the courtroom change.

> MC
> Nobody wants to have to go through this. We'll get
> charges dropped.

Mc turns toward Sydney.

> MC
> Sorry I didn't call you yesterday. I got tied up.

                    SYDNEY
          Oh, so that's what your into now. I saw you on TV
          last night. And this morning.

                    SYDNEY
          I thought we were through with heater cases.

                    MC
          How can I be? Maybe if it weren't two children being
          lied on, I might not be involved. I'm just glad to
          see you decided to join me. Anyway I deposited nine
          thousand into the account this morning.

MC looked over at RODNEY LAWSON, the other lawyer the men hired to work with them on the case. He is busy at a laptop.

                    MC
          What's that you're working on?

                    RODNEY
          I thought I'd start outlining points of the case
          now, as it happens. I have a feeling we're going to
          need an edge or two.

MC nodded but in disbelieve.

All stood as the bailiff called the court to order. MC takes his place near the bench opposite of the prosecutors.

                    JUDGE 1
          Bailiff, bring those two boys out first.

The bailiff calls the children's names and they enter the courtroom, dwarfed by six Sheriff Deputies.

All that can be heard is soft crying in tandem. The men stood aside and revealed their small prisoners dressed in wrinkled, stained clothing. Whispers rippled through the courtroom.

The judge ordered the prosecutors to read the state's evidence against the boys.

It charged them with the execution-style torture death of Toyman.

                    MC
          Judge, you will find that there is no probable cause

to hold these boys--these babies, in the county lock-
up. I ask the court to release them to their parents
as they are not a flight risk. They are honor
students and often cleaned up near and around
Toyman's store.

          LEAD PROSECUTOR
Your Honor, we have witness statements placing both
young men at the scene of the crime and both of them
confessed to detectives, Crowe and Marrsec that they
used a brick to knock Toyman unconscious, dragged
him to the vacant lot and tortured him until he
died.

Mc handed the clerk papers which requested permission to see any evidence the state had against his clients

          MC
Your, honor I respectfully request from the State, a
list of his witnesses they have interviewed, police
reports and any other proof they may have against my
clients. I also request you allow the children to be
released to their parents until the next court date.

The prosecutors discuss amongst themselves.

          LEAD PROSECUTOR
Your Honor, the State does not have the documents
Mr.Combs is requesting, in its possession.

          MC
Judge, I ask that this court postpone this hearing
until the State can produce the documents I am
requesting and let the boys be released into the
custody of their parents.

The judge scratches his head.

          JUDGE 1
We will precede on schedule, gentlemen. The court
finds probable cause to hold these boys in the
county lock up each on ten million dollars bond.
Counselor, I'm setting the next court date for next
month. Bailiff, can you call the next prisoner
please?

Mc turned to watch the guards walk the sobbing boys back to the jail.

He turned around to see the faces of his partners, the boys' mothers, and horde of spectators and reporters. He turned to look at the little boys but couldn't see them. He could only hear the wails of the small boys.

He glanced over his shoulder at the press. He walked right towards Lois as she scooted through the emptying courtroom toward him.

He didn't immediately see the other seven reporters walking towards him too. He took a breath and started to smile.

          LOIS
That wasn't a good thing that happened for the defense was it? What next?

Lois jammed her tape recorder right under MC's nose and for a moment he paused.

          MC
I thought they didn't allow tape recorders in the courtroom? Why don't we continue the interviews outside of the courtroom.

          LEAD PROSECUTOR
Yes, we should move this into the hallway.

EXT: COURTROOM HALLWAY

The press and camera operators gather around the prosecutors outside of the courtroom. Mc and Sydney walked outside of the courtroom discussing strategy. Wilma and Gina approach the two lawyers.

          WILMA
I though you were going to stop this? Why are the boys still in jail...what's going on here?

          MC
This hearing was just a formality. It only means they were formally charged with the crime, that there was enough evidence to hold the boys.

He took the ladies off to the side holding on to their shoulders unprepared for this type of speech.

          MC

> Ladies, we're going to talk to the press now. We'll sit down and discuss strategy later tonight. Lady 1, I can see the tears welling up in your eyes, that's good. Lady 2, you look angry, that's good too. Use it for the cameras. Let the people know how you feel.

Pushing the women towards the waiting press, Third chair and Second chair stayed behind to watch MC's classic maneuvers.

> RODNEY
> I hear how he's spinning it to the parents but how are we going to get those children out of jail?

> SYDNEY
> After the cameras stop rolling, we'll see a different atmosphere and we'll get them out of jail.

> RODNEY
> Better do something, quick.

MC walked Lady1 and Lady2 towards the waiting press.

> LOIS
> Prosecutor 1, why, is it that you denied MC evidence in this case.

She shoved her tape recorder in the man's face as all of the bright camera lights illuminated the group.

> LEAD PROSECUTOR
> There is a way things work...

The prosecutor was interrupted by Gina

> GINA
> You are torturing two innocent children. How could you believe to small boys could drag a man of that size one half mile?

The debates on the finer points of the case went on for 20 minutes with MC garnering the support of the community and the disdain of the state. Prosecutor 1 ended his comments to the press.

> LEAD PROSECUTOR

> We will release a written statement this afternoon ladies and gentlemen. That is all.

The prosecutors walked away from the group.

> **LEAD PROSECUTOR**
> Why is that man always trying to prosecute the State?

> **PROSECUTOR 2**
> He's a defense attorney.

MC, Sydney and Rodney stand outside of the courtroom to make lunch plans.

> **MC**
> I know you had wanted to take the easy way out of the case by pleading guilty and getting it over with, because you felt I was only handling the case to please the old neighborhood. I'm was still in touch with my roots. Anyway, the practice has lost two clients in the past few years and we needed a win. Hopefully after a winning this case, you might stop whining about it. Think about it--a civil suit will take care of everything financially.

> **SYDNEY**
> It's not that everyone under the sun had not already sued the town, but it always seemed if our cases lately are aimed at police or prosecutorial misconduct--something that is hard to get a judge to see and even harder to get an editor to print. I don't want to limit my choices, MC.

Lois interrupts their conversation.

> **LOIS**
> Hey, you sounded pretty good up there--for once, she said.

> **MC**
> Who me? Miss uh whass your name again?

> **LOIS**
> Ha Ha. Laugh now because I hear the prosecution has a surprise witness to the murder.

                    MC
Where'd you hear that from? MC said, folding his
arms across his chest.

                    LOIS
Around. O.K. see you later. I gotta catch up with
the prosecution. Besides it might get dangerous
being seen with you, Mr. Public Enemy number one,

Flashing her pretty smile-- she began to walk away.

                    MC
I guess we'll see about that, Miss Reporter, he said
relaxing his tone a bit.

Sydney looked slightly offended that she had not offered him the same
smile when he spoke to her.

                    SYDNEY
 I guess you're still the only lawyer she sees
standing here.

                    MC
Yup. Just the way I like it.

The three lawyers stood apart from the crowd comparing women's body parts
as they walked by--smiling.

                    RODNEY
You better get your mind on your business before you
don't have one.

                    SYDNEY
Before we don't have one.

                    MC
I got mine together-- and it would be even better if
I could top it off with some good food. Where are we
going to eat?

 Second chair slipped a look in Lois' direction and then in the direction
of Prosecutor 1.

                    SYDNEY
Go find out what she knows.

                    MC
Why do I have to talk to her. I don't need too.

                    MC
Now, I might go talk to some of them.

                    SYDNEY
O.K. if you say so. But I was talking about you finding out what and who she knows for once. She owes us that at the very least.

MC looked at him in disbelieve.

                    MC
Why would I want to find out what she knows. She doesn't know anything more than any other big-boobed reporter.

                    SYDNEY
I'm serious. I hear she's awfully cozy with several of the prosecutors and the feds now that she's not ringing your phone off the hook anymore. I wonder what kind of new friends she's made since then.

Second chair started walking toward the elevator and Third chair followed.

                    SYDNEY
Better do something.

                    MC
Damn the press, anyway. What this town needs is a good shaking,

                    SYDNEY
Don't shake too hard --you have to live in this town too, you know.

MC looked but didn't respond. He followed the men onto the elevator.

INT: THE ELEVATOR

                    RODNEY
The judge doesn't really want to hear this case anyway. She's doing me a favor for getting her son out of that mess with police two years ago...

RODNEY
We need to win this. I know I'm not a partner--yet--
but Marshman, Fallow, and Kapp just got the Tellman
case, you know. The one where the guy was driving on
a suspended license and accidentally got shot in the
head by police? MC said.

MC
UNHUMM.

SYDNEY
But it was no accident. Seems he owed the wrong
people money and had a big mouth. He went to wrong
kind of police thinking he would get protection and
word got out. But that's them-- I know we need to
concentrate on winning this. This is just as big--
even bigger.

The men exit the elevator. Second chair slipped a look in Lois' direction and then in the direction of the Prosecutor 1. Lois walked outside

MC
Hey, I'll meet you two back here in a few minutes.

MC walks outside catching up with Lois

MC
I saw you over there bothering my clients. What did
you ask them?

LOIS
They wouldn't talk. They said their lawyer
instructed them not to talk to anyone, she said.

MC
Right. And you want?

LOIS
To talk with them exclusively, to get their side of
the story,

MC
You only talk to me when you need some information.
If it were not for this case you wouldn't be
bothered with me. Just last week, you walked right

past me without speaking and now you want an
exclusive. What do I get out of it? MC said.

          LOIS
Please stop acting like a little bitch. Stop trying
to get something all of the time.

MC just glared at her.

          MC
I see why your husband left you. And no you cannot
interview my clients today or any other time.

          MC
Remember that time I gave you my business card and
wrote my pager number on the back of it? I wish I
could take that moment back because I think you have
the wrong idea about me. People do not address me
the way you do.

          LOIS
I'm sorry. I didn't mean to say bitch. It just came
out. You're difficult to deal with sometimes. How
about dinner? My treat, O.K. Say about 7:30
tonight?

          MC
Me? Go somewhere with you, so you can embarrass me?

          LOIS
Look I need a little bit of background--the easy
way. Now, I know I taught you better than to pass
up a lobster dinner from a pretty woman..

          MC
 You know I'm still married,

          LOIS
Yeah, to a woman who lives across the street from
you, right. Or are you referring to that little
chippy buzzing about at that rally on your mother's
front porch?

          MC
Whatever. How'd you find out about all of that?

LOIS
Hell, everyone knows everyone else's business in this little bitty place. Just like you know my husband left me--I know that little home wrecker you've been rolling around with was the cause of your loving wife moving out. Besides, I don't want to marry you, just pick you brain a little. I need this story, MC. I don't want to be stuck in this place forever.

MC
O.K. 7:30. Oh, yeah don't get any ideas. I didn't mean to touch you there,

Mc fingered the lapel of her suit coat.

MC
This is nice, where'd you get it?

LOIS

You remembered? she said smiling.

MC
7:30.

Mc walks away.

SYDNEY
I see you talked to her. What did she say?

MC
We're going out later. Nothing serious, why do you ask? That woman is not my problem--she's her husband's problem--I guess.

SYDNEY
Well she must have gotten you pretty steamed up you walked away mumbling.

MC
When that woman first started in this city--I can hardly describe it. O k. Eclectic. Colorful. Country. Pick one

SYDNEY

>So you took her on one of your famous shopping trips
>where you show the poor thing what to wear...

Sydney's voice trails off into a sigh, looking bored with MC's ego.

>MC
>I already got a wife who hates me and I'm not
>looking for another worry. Questions?

>SYDNEY
>Nothing--no, I'm cool. I was just asking. Let's go
>eat. My wife and I found a great new gourmet soul
>food restaurant in the next town last week. Rodney,
>are you coming?

>RODNEY
> No, I'm going to hang around here and get something
>to eat.

Rodney motioned towards one of the smiling, big-butt, women they had gawked at earlier.

>SYDNEY
>Okay.

INT. LOCAL SOUL FOOD RESTAURANT-DAY

The two men enter the restaurant. Soft jazz is playing in the background.

>SYDNEY
>Ya know, our buddy, Slick? well he is in some sort
>of trouble. it seems as if his dealings have
>attracted the attention of some local gangsters and
>he got to talking and to make a long story short,
>The gangsters now want a piece of the action with
>the night jobs and stuff. They paid a little visit
>to my house yesterday. That's what I was talking
>about in the courtroom.

MC stopped mid-chew on his fried pork chop sandwich.

SERIES OF SHOTS:

A)Movers taking law degree off of his office wall and dismantling the furniture.

B) Standing in front of his family with his pockets turned inside out.

C) Imagining himself, like Sal, scrubbing urinals.

>SYDNEY
>Are you ok?

MC just sat there with a wad of half-chewed sandwich in his mouth. Staring.

>SYDNEY
>It'll be alright. Swallow.

MC started chewing his sandwich slowly.

>MC
>No it won't, This game we've been playing is now a case. We're lawyers. Sydney. We can't break the law. Do you really think Slick would stand up for either one of us? He still hasn't paid us for that misdemeanor last year. Remember when he shot that woman's pit bull?

MC puts his sandwich down and rubs his forehead.

>MC
>I can't believe the only thing holding my career together right now is Slick's ass. Damn.

>SYDNEY
>I know. Look I gotta plan....

>MC
>No plans.

>SYDNEY
>Then what?

>MC
>We'll give 'em a piece of the action--hell they can run the whole damn thing. All we have to do is find replacements for us. Anyone else who wants to be connected with it can still do it. Slick's in charge now since he's the cause of everything going awry.. Better let him know.

                    SYDNEY
What? this ain't a fight club ya know. I don't think
it'll be that easy.

                    MC:
No it won't but how else will we disassociate
ourselves from this? I went out with them last night
after Her left. Slick can handle it. He wants the
money anyway.

Sydney lowered his head and continued eating his meal.

INT: INSIDE THE NEWSROOM-DAY

The staff, heads bent, shoulders hunched over computer terminals, is busy putting together the next day's paper. Lois sits atop a desk cradling a phone. She hangs up and walks toward her editor's office.

                    LOIS
I think I'll take the suggestion to write that
series about this serial killer running around the
city. I'll need today and tomorrow--o.k.

                    FRANK
Sure, what about the two boys?

                    LOIS
Well, that case is taking more than it's share of
strange twists. I'll be meeting with the boys'
lawyer this evening.

                    FRANK
Who? Sydney?

                    LOIS
No, I'll be meeting with Martin Combs later this
evening about seven thirty-ish. Our treat-right?

                    FRANK
Yeah, Get receipts and just be careful because the
man is a defense attorney. Check out what he tells
you with the prosecutors.

                    LOIS
Thanks, Editor, I will. I'm stopping by police
headquarters first.

Lois smiles as Frank fans his hands and continues with his work. She grabs her gear and heads towards the door.

INSIDE HEADQUARTERS-DAY

> LOIS
> Hey, CLERK, is Detective Division Chief in?

> CLERK
> Yes, Lois, is he expecting you?

> LOIS
> Yes, he's this weeks' exclusive

> CLERK LAUGHS
> O.k. Honey. Have a seat.

The Clerk phones the Chief's office.

> CLERK
> You can go back.

Lois grabs her gear and goes back to the office.

> CHIEF
> Glad you could come, Lois. Let me give you a tour
> and introduce you to the staff

Lois puts her things in the Chief's office and pulls out her reporter's notebook.

> LOIS
> How many woman have been identified so far, chief?

> CHIEF
> You don't waste time do you, Lois.

> LOIS
> Well, it's just that I'm on deadline.

> CHIEF
> O.K. We'll skip the introductions.

The chief goes into his office, sits down and pulls up some information on his laptop.

                    CHIEF
          Lois, you're not squeamish, are you?

                    LOIS
          No, go ahead.

                    CHIEF
          Most of these murders have gone into our cold case
          file but we have captured at least three of the
          suspects. One sits on death row. Keep that in mind
          while you're looking at these photos.

The Chief turns around the laptop. Lois' eyes stare in horror as she flips through photographs of the women left behind by a serial killer who preys on prostitutes and drug addicts.

The crime scene photographs showed the women dead and naked left in trash pile heaps and one left in a lewd position inside a church. Lois turned the computer towards the Chief virtually unshaken.

                    LOIS
          I've seen enough. Was this supposed to scare me?

                    CHIEF
          No, just to inform you of what we are dealing with.
          Some of these women had been on the streets for most
          of their lives. For the past ten years we've been
          tracking several of these killers and quite frankly
          all of the ones we have caught are from the same
          urban neighborhood as the Toyman was found.

                    LOIS
          Do you think Toyman was one of the serial murder's
          victims?

                    CHIEF
          I cannot comment further on that case because it's
          still open. Here these documents may be useful.

The Chief hands Lois a folder of information.

                    LOIS
          I can use this for my article?

                    CHIEF

Yes.

The Chief and Lois sit in uncomfortable silence for a few seconds. Lois begins to gather her things.

>   LOIS
> Well, I probably have more than enough for the article. Can I call you tomorrow if I have more questions?

>   CHIEF
> Sure, Lois

The detective gets up and shows Lois to the door. Lois gathers her things and head towards her car. Once she's inside her car, she starts to cry. She pulls out of the parking lot and heads towards the restaurant where she agreed to meet MC. She puts in her favorite CD and turns it up loudly, still crying.

EXT: LOCAL RESTAURANT ON OUTSKIRTS OF TOWN-NIGHT

Lois pulls into the parking lot. Looking in her vanity mirror, trying to salvage her face she daubs on more lipstick, eye shadow and mascara. Unbeknownst to her, MC had arrived early and was watching her from his car a few spaces down. Eventually, Lois gets out of her car and heads toward the restaurant. Before she can get to the door, MC rolls down his window and loudly calls LOIS.

>   MC
> In a hurry?

>   LOIS
> No, I thought you would be late.

MC opens his car doors motioning for Lois to get inside. She slides into the car, butt first.

>   MC
> Now, have you ever known me to be late?

>   LOIS
> Yes.

MC faces forward in his car. The pair sits in comfortable silence. He fiddles with the radio dial turning away from the smooth jazz.

LOIS
Are you nervous or something

MC
No, why.

LOIS
You're fidgeting with the radio.

MC
I though you liked rap music.

LOIS
We really don't know each other personally, do we?

MC
No, we don't

LOIS
I like rap and jazz. Let's go inside, I'm hungry.

MC and Lois get out of the car and head toward the nearly deserted restaurant.

MC
I hope this is a good place. I've never been here before.

LOIS
Yeah, it is. I'm glad you could make it.

MC
No, bid deal, it's just dinner.

The pair sits in a booth and order steaks.

MC
It's been a while since we've really sat down and talked

LOIS
Yeah, I've been busy keeping up with the case and the serial killings and all.

MC
Lois, I know you didn't invite me here just to talk

about the case.

LOIS
Yeah, I did. We can discuss the case, work, whatever but honestly, I'm a little worn out now. We don't have to.

MC
I figured I had that case sewed up. I mean I had already made plans on what to do with the money.

LOIS
What's you're retainer fee?

MC
Fifteen hundred but it's more now. Lois, Everyone knows those two little boys--any kids that young-- could pull off something like that. Kids that age can't do much of anything except play.

LOIS
But Toyman was a pretty well know figure in the neighborhood. The whole thing is strange MC. Who would want to hurt a man who gave away toys to children.

MC
Maybe that's why the police haven't caught the killer yet. That probable cause hearing was a sham. When I went back to where they were being held I couldn't even see 'em. All I heard was crying. At least they have the kids separated from the other inmates.

LOIS
Yeah, they wouldn't put kids in general pop.

MC
At least. And that is the very least they could do. I cannot see two little boys jumping bail.

LOIS
What did you find out about the cops who made the arrest.

MC

They both have past instances of making up stuff about kids.

> LOIS
> What? They really don't seem that way. I talk to those two almost every day.

> MC
> You do?

MC stared at Lois. The waitress returned with their meals.

> LOIS
> They're still cops and I am a police reporter. I have to talk to them if I want any information.

> MC
> If I have anything to do with it, they won't be cops for long. Crooks should be crooks and cops should be cops--not liars.

> LOIS
> The district cops were looking for an adult male anyway, not two little boys.

> MC
> My point exactly. I wonder why Dirty Cop 1 and Dirty Cop 2 stepped in and started looking for two kids. When you look at the police reports, there were other detectives working the case and they were looking for an adult. They released a composite of an adult male. That so-called confession they beat out of those kids can't be the only thing that their arrest is based on but I don't have any proof of that--just that the boys weren't the murders. For one thing they aren't physically able to pull it off.

> LOIS
> Unhun.

> MC
> Guess I ought to find out, huh? Maybe I can find out something about the red car Toyman was last seen in. The police arrested those guys but for some reason, but that along with a few other police reports that

are not being made available to me, are either incomplete or missing according to the state.

          LOIS
Yeah, I sorta read a few of them and the detectives placed the victim in a car and then something about being seen walking down the street with another adult. MC, this case is strange. One would thing the assistant state's attorney would at least be cooperative, considering the age of the boys. I hear they're planning to move them to a mental institution for safe keeping.

          MC
Really? Where'd you hear all of this from.

          LOIS
Around. Now, who was the woman I saw you with at the press conference?

          MC
What woman? I know you aren't talking about HER.

          LOIS
Yeah, Superman, Her. What was up with the attitude? It's not like she's your wife or anything.

MC wipes his mouth and stretches out his arms.

          MC
Since we're on the subject of mates, where is Tyrone?

Lois pauses for a moment, fork mid-air, and glares at MC

          LOIS
Who? I know you aren't referring to my husband.

Lois looks up at him waiting for a response.

          MC
Yes, I am.

          LOIS
I don't know where my husband is. And I'm not looking for him anymore.

Lois continues to eat. MC starts on his meal again, swollen with confidence.

          LOIS
Look, the man doesn't want a wife and responsibilities of two kids, so he I split from this virtual dope house he had us living in, moved in with my parents and then into an apartment. Since then he's been drifting in and out. Staying out all night--I even caught him once. I don't even know why he moved us back up here. He's a fucking headache and a half. Now you know.

          MC
I didn't need to know all of that. And you should stop cussing. It's not lady like.

          LOIS
I do a lot of things that aren't lady like.

MC continues to eat his meal.

          LOIS
Before coming here, I interviewed the Lead Detective for this city. He showed me photo after photo of naked, dead women--victims of this serial murder running rampant--who where left dead in lewd positions. I must have viewed 50 or so photographs. Then he mentioned the series on your case. He said the women come from the same neighborhood that Toyman was found murdered in.

          MC
Crime scene photos, huh?

          LOIS
It's not what he said, it's what he didn't say. I got an eerie feeling from the whole thing.

          MC
 Maybe you should get a new beat. Write about something else.

          LOIS
What else is there MC. Why should I be the one to

hide away--I haven't done anything wrong. Look, I
understand some of the pressures police are under,
they don't get paid enough to do what they do. The
question is: how am I affecting their job. I talk to
the public. I get paid to tell them what is going on
while they are at work. That's what I do. That is
what I love. More than an iffy archaic husband or
someone's opinion of me or anything. Don't you get
to do what you love to do? Why shouldn't I. I paid
my debt to society--I am raising two children damn
near by myself. That's my debt.

    MC
I hear you. Why don't you just divorce him?

    LOIS
That's another story altogether. The man told me
long ago he would fake his death before he would pay
a dime in child support. I should have taken that as
a hint and cut my losses but I didn't. I really
didn't know any better then, but now that I'm
getting older...Hell, he can win this battle.
Every time I mention it he blows up. I kinda think he
just wants a home base and we're it. I just don't
want my little boy growing up to mimic his lax ways.
I will give him this much--he taught me a lot. I'm
not physically nor mentally able to be a fool
anymore. Hell, I'm just tired of the bullshit.

    MC
I would be too, If I were you. I see why my subtle
sexual overtures didn't quite go over with you.

    LOIS
I didn't mean to burden you. I know your plate must
be already full enough with the case and all.

    MC
You still love him don't you?

    LOIS
Yeah, why shouldn't I. But just because you love
someone doesn't mean that you like 'em or can live
with "em. You just love 'em.

    MC

>   I like that, what you just said. It pretty much sums
>   it up. A person should find someone they like and
>   can live with and then love them.

Lois for once during the meal just looked at MC without speaking or eating.

>   MC
> What?

>   LOIS
> Nothing, I'm just looking at you.

>   MC
> Lois, can I ask you a serious question?

>   LOIS
> Sure.

>   MC
> Can you dance?

>   LOIS
> Yes, sir I can

>   MC
> Good. Let's meet Rodney at Slick's. I can follow you
> home to drop off your car. I know you like to sip a
> little and you sound like you could use a little
> break.

Smiling, Lois brushes her ankle against MC's leg underneath the table. MC smiles bashfully and they continue their meal in comfortable silence.

INT: SLICK'S MIRAGE-NIGHT

SLICK and G-Man's sidekick, CRANE is inside the crowded nightclub watching the crowd enjoy the party.

>   SLICK
> So, how're we going to do this. I sure this comes
> with set rates far below the norm.

>   CRANE
> That's not your concern. Just do as I say. Where is
> your office.

The men walk up a spiral staircase leading to Slick's office as MC, Lois and Rodney show up at the night club to catch a new R&B cover band.

          RODNEY
Maybe someone ought to go tell Slick about the new arrangement.

          MC
You mean me?

          RODNEY
Yeah. I'll make sure Lois isn't paying attention. Just go take care of that before it gets out of hand.

MC'S FLASHBACK-TALKING TO SLICK

          MC
We can organize an escort service that was open to high end clients--women. With money.

          SLICK
Yeah, we can have all kinds of clients. Old, young, swingers, transvestites. You know what they say: There is someone for everyone.

          SLICK
The only thing have to have in common is money. was they were all loaded with money. Old money.

          MC
We made an exception for you Slick.

          SYDNEY
We felt that you wouldn't go for all of this. I mean you do alright with the club and all.

          SLICK
I can always use more money.

END FLASHBACK

BACK TO PRESENT DAY

INT: SLICK'S MIRAGE-NIGHT

MC pulled Third Chair aside.

          MC
Slick is the cause of all of this unraveling

          RODNEY
Slick is a man like any other and he had needs--just like we did. He needed money excitement and sex. Who else could we get to help us to do something stupid like this.

          MC
I knew he made his money through staging fraudulent insurance claims-- but I thought he knew where to spread the cash.

          RODNEY
Maybe he left someone out.

          MC
The only reason I said yes is because he was never caught or questioned--until now.

          RODNEY
Second said a guy named Tunks sent him a calling card--I don't know how he found out.

          MC
Well, he told me Slick had some people coming down on him about it.

          RODNEY
Maybe. I wasn't there and you weren't either.

          MC
Most of the who's who in the town were clients and they all seemed to stick together on the notion of keeping their club hush-hush. Word got around with the ladies quick and we began to prosper. We were making a lot of money.

          RODNEY
Come on MC we never intended anything like this. I didn't get home until 4:30 a.m. And that woman had to be kicking 60 in the butt with a steel toe boot.

                    MC
I bet you everyone wasn't getting a fur coat out of
the deal. I'm willing to bet all of this fell apart
thanks to somebody's disgruntled wife. And no I
never thought it would get to this point.

                    RODNEY
Yeah, living in a resort town has its advantages.
There is always a stream of something willing to pay
for anything. All we had to do was entertain a few
ladies. Nothing fancy, just escort them to whatever
function they were going to and if they were special
and were paying more, they would get a little more.
It seemed simple.

Mc approached Slick and Crane as they headed up the stairs.

                    CRANE
Whoa, You're MC aren't you--the ones getting the
boys out of jail. I saw you on TV.

                    MC
Yeah, I'm the one.

                    CRANE
Yeah, G-man really appreciates this, you know.

                    MC
Who?

                    CRANE
The man who pays you--G-Man? Oh, maybe you know him
as Gerald. I hear you all go way back.

                    MC
Yeah... Slick, can I speak to you for a moment?

                    SLICK
I'm kinda busy, can it wait?

MC looks at both men.

                    MC
Yeah, I'm over there near the stage.

MC pulls Rodney away from the table.

> MC
>
> Did you see that guy who was with Slick? He just told me that basically I'm working for one of the biggest criminals in North America. If I remember correctly, he has links to organized crime. No wonder Sydney got a visit paid to him. That Slick has one of G-Man's friends in his office right now.
>
> RODNEY
>
> What do we do now--leave?
>
> MC
>
> Naw, I'm talking to Slick tonight. This will end now. I, apparently, am getting the two boys out of all of this, for G-man, for some strange reason.

MC and Rodney return to where Lois is sitting.

> LOIS
>
> MC, sit here.

She motions for MC to sit next to her. He sits down, unsettled by the conversation he had but Lois runs her hand up his leg and places her arm on the back of his chair.

> MC
>
> Lois, I might have to drop you off earlier than I expected. I just wanted to let you know.
>
> LOIS
>
> MC, have a drink or something. Why are you so tense?

MC looks at Lois for a second before leaning over and kissing her. Then he puts his arm around her waist.

> MC
>
> Do you know anyone named, G-Man?
>
> LOIS
>
> Yeah, I met him at the uh...rally. I think I still have his card.

Lois starts to ramble through her bag. She produces G-man's business card which states that he is a private detective. She gives it to MC.

                    LOIS
            Why did you kiss me.

                    MC
            I don't know. I just wanted to.

MC hugs her a little and plants a kiss on her forehead.

                    MC
            Let's just watch the band.

MC puts the card in his inner pocket.

ACT II

INT. TRIAL COURT--TWO WEEKS LATER

MC entered the courtroom hurriedly, and sat next to his tiny clients. His partners were already seated.

Nervous chatter fills the courtroom along with a hushed murmur as the judge approached the bench.

                    TRIAL JUDGE
            Will the prosecution begin opening statements?

                    LEAD PROSECUTOR
            Yes your honor.

MC leaned over towards second chair as Lead Prosecutor drones on in the background.

                    MC
            The only thing they'll hear is a bunch of white
            lies. Did you bring the photographs? second chair
            pointed to the huge white-backed posters they were
            to use during their presentation.

                    SYDNEY
            So what did you do last night?

                    MC
            Last night? Oh, I went to Slick's with Lois and
            Rodney.

                    SYDNEY

How was it?

>   MC
> How was what?

Sydney gives MC a look and snickers.

>   MC
> Don't start, Sydney. That's why Rodney was there--to make sure I didn't do anything stupid.

>   TRIAL JUDGE
> We'll take a 30 minute recess so Mr. Combs can get himself together,

>   MC
> Oh no, I'm fine your honor.

>   TRIAL JUDGE
> Are you sure sir?

>   MC
> Yes.

Lead Prosecutor finished his opening statement.

MC shook his head as he rose from his chair, positioning his silk tie into his wool Ralph Lauren suit jacket.

The smiles and stares he got from the female jurors--and the gay man sitting on the end, attested to his charm.

>   MC
> Your honor, ladies and gentlemen of the jury, my statement, as well will be brief but of an entirely different nature. Please, look at the two little boys sitting at the table. They're drawing pictures. Let me show you.

MC swiftly approached the table and inched the colorful drawings away from the children.

>   LEAD PROSECUTOR
> Objection, your honor.

He held the drawings up for the room to view. He motioned to the judge for permission to pass them around. She nodded.

          MC
What do you see here? I see pictures of the Power Rangers and of dogs and a picture on this particular sheet, of a police officer with a gun in his hand. Now, if you or I were on trial for our lives, would we sit quietly drawing mindlessly? No we wouldn't. And neither would these boys if they were aware of what they are facing--life imprisonment. But what you get to decide is: does the prosecution has enough evidence to do that.

MC whirled around, surveying the room and demonstrating the courtroom theatrics he's known for.

          MC
I say you'll find they do not. Not just because the boys were snatched out of their homes, dragged down to the police station--at least four times--and lied on in the middle of the night All without their parents, or a lawyer present. All of this ladies and gentlemen based on a confession. Detectives Victor Crowe and Theodore Marrsec. The kids' words against theirs.

          MC
That's what is needed to convict someone of a crime-- evidence. Not a weak confession beat out of two children--the police have to show factually what the physical evidence says. Not what the confession says. Because it doesn't matter. It's a false confession that these grown men beat and harassed out of my clients--who are children in every since of the word.

          LEAD PROSECUTOR
Objection, your honor,

          TRIAL JUDGE
Overruled. You may continue counselor.

          MC
Thank you, your honor. I said I wouldn't keep you and I won't-- I know you're hungry. I am too. But I want a little justice with my lunch today. Because

tomorrow they'll be coming after your boys and your
girls. Your niece, nephew--this has to stop. This is
not how law enforcement professionals behave. It is
how criminals act, though. I should know, I've
defended a few of them.

Mc looks at two men located in the rear of the courtroom.

> MC
> Now consider the credibility of the two men who are
> acting as detectives, afraid to tell the truth about
> who they found really killed this man, one of our
> prominent citizens. Early in the investigation they
> were looking at two grown men then suddenly they're
> at the boys homes every other week. Are they afraid
> because there was maybe a grudge to settle? Afraid
> to tell because they fear for their jobs or maybe
> they're just lazy and figured no one would care. Is
> it that these boys have to suffer for the sin of
> poverty? Maybe the police always know who rapes and
> ravages in that neighborhood. My God, these men are
> seasoned detectives who know how to find evidence.
> They know all of the players! Maybe the two men
> acting as detectives get paid to do what they do on
> both ends--by you the taxpayer and then again by
> their real bosses. That group of thugs sitting over
> there in the corner, hoping to intimidate you by
> being here.

Mc points at Hoodlum, who is sitting with several of his friends.

> MC
> But don't worry, one of them has an open federal
> warrant hanging over his head and he doesn't even
> know it. They can't hurt you.

Everyone in the courtroom turns around and whispers

> TRIAL JUDGE
> Mr. Combs, please restrict your comments to this
> case.

> MC
> Yes your honor.

Mc looks at a group of uniformed officers in the back of the courtroom.

                    MC
I'm afraid of them. They'll lie on anybody to close
a case. Just like they're lying on my clients,
today. And on you or your loved ones tomorrow.
Unless, when you retire to the jury chambers to
decide the fate of two kids that can't even keep
their noses wiped, you uphold your oath to God and
to this court to consider the evidence only, and not
the hearsay from the prosecution's witnesses about
what they think they heard--because none of them
actually say they saw the boys commit the crime when
the police say it happened. You'll even find the
children, along with several others, were all across
the street from the crime scene that whole week---
and that whole day the man's body was found.

            LEAD PROSECUTOR
Objection.

            TRIAL JUDGE
Overruled

                    MC
Thank you

Mc turns away from the jurors and returns to his seat. Then the lead prosecutor stood up to give his closing statements.

Some of the jurors mumbled because they thought they were going to get to lunch.

MC glanced up at his former clients he used as examples seated in the courtroom. They all worked their night jobs together,

MC pulled four brand new Power Rangers out of his coat pocket and handed them to the boys. He sat down between the children. He stretched his long, muscular legs underneath the table and relaxed in his chair as Lead Prosecutor droned on.

SERIES OF SHOTS: MC'S DAYDREAM

A) Lois and MC kiss

B) Share a dinner of strawberries and fresh cream in his hot tub.

C) Tumble into his round bed covered in satin sheets and rose petals

C) Herra is standing outside his door banging loudly and waking the neighbors with his angry wife in tow.

D) In a state of shot he sits up in the bed.

END SERIES--BACK TO COURTROOM

The Bailiff's baritone voice startled him. He had not even heard the prosecution's re-direct.

    BAILIFF (OFF-CAMERA)
"All rise."

    TRIAL JUDGE
  We can all meet back here at 1:30 this afternoon. Is
  that a good time counselors?

The men nodded in agreement.

Everyone agreed and begun to file out of the courtroom. Although opening arguments were a mini accomplishment, He approached Gina and Wilma and whispered something to them.

The women nodded in agreement and walked away. MC saw his former clients standing in front of the courthouse when the doors opened.

    MC
  Hey, I'll meet you two outside, he said.

They watched him approach the gentlemen outside.

    HOODLUM
  O.K. Ironsides, the federal warrant was made up
  right? hoodlum said.

    MC
  Well, sort of..

    HOODLUM
  Sort of what? Hoodlum said.

    MC
  You had an open federal warrant but I took care of
  it. When was the last time you checked in with your

probation officer?

    HOODLUM
Oh you mean Big Butt? She put me out.

    MC
What are you talking about, 'put you out'?

    HOODLUM
Well we kind of hooked up, you know me. But then we kind of fell out. She didn't want me to go anywhere. She was still acting like my probation officer.

    MC
She still IS your probation officer. Look, just give her a call. I guess she just wanted to see where you were. I guess you've been busy lately.

    MC
Ah love. Here, you guys enjoy a ball game or two on me,

MC handed both of the men season passes to the basketball game.

    OFFICER 1
Yeah, I was wondering when the good part was going to get here.

    MC
Oh no, I wouldn't do that to you for nothing. Enjoy. And please, Hoodlum, call your woman,'

    HOODLUM
Definitely.

    MC
By the way, you should call Slick for all of your personal business from now on.

The men nodded to MC but didn't respond.

INT:INSIDE THE NEWSROOM-DAY

Lois strides into the newsroom, coat open, fluttering behind her briefcase in hand.

> RECEPTIONIST
> The editor wants to see you.

> LOIS
> Is it good or bad?

> RECEPTIONIST
> I couldn't tell. He has some other people in his office too. Suits.

> LOIS'
> Okay thanks.

Lois places her briefcase and coat down on her desk and heads back to her editor's office.

> FRANK
> Lois, I'd like for you to meet Agent 1 and Agent 2

> LOIS
> Good morning gentlemen what can I do you for?

> FRANK
> This is serious Lois. You might be in danger.

> AGENT 1
> Lois, our office has received information that one of the articles you wrote about the two young boys has attracted the attention of some local underworld types.

> AGENT 2
> These types of people read the paper too. It seems they would like to know who your sources are.

> LOIS
> How did the federal government come into play in all of this?

> AGENT 1
> These are criminals under surveillance. I cannot tell you any more accept that we've assigned a few men to keep tabs on you.

> LOIS
> So what am I supposed to do? Hide--stay home or

what?

> AGENT 2
> Yeah, all we can say at this point that you'll be safe. We can't tell you much more than that. You can go about your normal routine.

> LOIS
> Ok, I guess.

> AGENT 1
> We've alerted you family and friends also. We'll brief the staff after this meeting. You may not be the only reporter in danger. There are a few others and we've alerted all of the news agencies in town.

> LOIS
> This is serious.

Both of the agents agree with her and begin to pack up their briefcases. The men exit the small office, leaving Lois and her editor in silence.

> FRANK
> Another thing Lois, I don't want you working on crime or political stuff anymore. Why don't you try the health beat. I-I mean really--how many stories do we need of MC and his heater cases. People don't want to read about that. Now, where to get a flu shot? Readers like that stuff.

> LOIS
> Yeah Frank. I guess I've finally been put on that railroad outta town, huh? I've heard much about it lately.

Lois rubs her forehead. She's slumped down in her chair. Editor avoids eye-contact and silence prevails. Editor concentrates on the parking lot outside of the window.

> FRANK
> Look, the Health beat is ok. It's better than nothing.

> LOIS
> This is hard to comprehend. What kind of town is this?

> FRANK
> Lois worse things can happen. Remember when I offered you a position on the desk? You didn't seem too interested in that, kiddo. My hands are tied now--I can't help you, it's too late. You're a young women with kids and a husband. How long did you think this super-reporter thing would last? Do you know how far some of your stories have reached? Did you notice that people are beginning to pay more attention to politics now. You helped with that. Hey--didn't just last week the S prosecutor's office tell you that you were beginning to sway public opinion?

Frank waited for Lois to look up. When she did, he met her gaze. It signaled the end of their meeting.

> LOIS
> I thought that was a good thing, Frank.

Lois began to gather her things and leave the office. All she wanted to do was eat.

> FRANK
> Sometimes it is, kiddo. But not here--not now.

Frank walks over to his desk, anxious to sit down.

> FRANK
> Close that on the way out, will ya.

Lois closes the door as she leaves, its symbolism recognizable only to her. She put on her smiley face just long enough to walk through the newsroom and head down to the cafeteria.

Frank throws a few antacids into his mouth and calls a number.

> FRANK
> ...Yeah, look she took it pretty hard but she's off the story--all of them.

INT: TUNK'S CAR

> TUNKS
> Okay.

Frank hears a click then hangs up the phone.

INT. CAFETERIA

Lois enters the newsroom cafeteria gets a crescent roll and takes a seat in the back of the busy eatery. With her head hung low, she began to pick at the crusty bread, brooding about her new situation. Co-worker 1 and 2 enter the cafe, eager to know what news Lois had encountered.

> CO-WORKER 1
> So, what did they say? You're not going to prison are you?

> LOIS
> Girl, naw. It's not like that. Ed just changed my beat. Now I can write about anything but crime and politics. I'm on the Health beat. It's cool.

> CO-WORKER 2
> Are we still meeting up at Slick's tonight?

> LOIS
> Yeah, girl don't play--I'm still the same old Lois.

> CO-WORKER 1
> Don't put that fake smile on for me 'cause I know you.

> LOIS
> Yeah, I know. But that's a good thing though, 'cause I really don't feel like smiling right now.

Lois pushed away from the table and made her way to the door. She got in her car and drove to see G-man.

INT:G-MAN OFFICE-DAY

Lois drove to G-man's office which was a part of the secluded warehouse where he had tortured Thug 1 and Thug 2. The unannounced visit was welcome. Gangster's office looked as if it had been professionally decorated. Crane is in the office and recognizes Lois from Slicks.

> LOIS
> Hey G-man, I hope you don't mind the intrusion.

> G-MAN
> Uh, no. Come on in. I don't have any clients scheduled today. What can I do you for.

Lois and G-man look at Crane

> G-MAN
> He's just leaving.

As Crane leaves, Lois is surveying the room, he notices articles about the boys scattered across a table in the office. Many of them are hers, along with some of the other cases she has been covering.

> LOIS
> I see you like to read.

Lois picks up one of her articles.

> G-MAN
> I like to keep up. I like the way emotion comes through in your writing. It's as if you really care.

> LOIS
> I do care. There's not much of a reason to do this outside of loving the field.

> LOIS
> Are you hungry? I know a little place we can get some lunch.

> G-MAN
> Yes, I am hungry. Where are we going?

> LOIS
> A little place I know, I'll surprise you.

The pair leaves the office and head to G-man's brand new SUV. Tunks is outside in his car watching the pair. He follows them.

> LOIS
> Nice truck.

> G-MAN
> You look familiar to me. Did you ever live in the south side neighborhood?

> LOIS
> Yeah, I did briefly.

> G-MAN
> You were pregnant then. I used to see you with a
> little girl. I though you looked so --I don't know
> how to describe it. Wholesome. You looked as if you
> weren't from around there.

> LOIS
> I'm not. I moved there with my husband. I'm from a
> neighboring state.

> G-MAN
> You're married?

> LOIS
> Yeah.

G-man didn't ask anything else about Lois' marriage and she didn't offer.
He looks in his rearview mirror and notices a car following him.

> G-MAN
> Where are we going? Some place quiet I hope. I'm not
> one for crowds.

> LOIS
> It's right here, pull over.

The two enter the restaurant. He notices Mobster's car still outside and
thinks of an excuse to leave.

> G-MAN
> We can't stay long, I have to go through some files
> back at the office.

> LOIS
> Can't stay long? Well I guess I'm the one who is out
> of sorts here. Since I barged in on you, it's ok if
> you leave now.

G-Man was all the while watching Mobster. He grabs Lois' arm and leads her
into the bistro. He seated them away from a window and near an exit.

> G-MAN
> We can stay a while.

G-Man beings to unfold his napkin and places it in his lap. He ordered automatically for both of them.

>LOIS
>I'm impressed. I'd thought you'd be more like the bachelor cop type. You're kinda smooth.

>G-MAN
>Thank you miss. Hey, let me ask you something: How's it going with the case of the two boys? MC getting along alright with the media?

>LOIS
>I don't know. I've been banished from covering crime. The FBI said it would be best if all of the press would cool it on the case. I guess they're looking into it now.

>G-MAN
>The FBI is looking at the case.

>LOIS
>Yeah, I guess. The real reason I asked you to lunch Gangster is that I'm trying to track down my husband.

Lois hands him a picture of the man.

>G-MAN
>Why are you asking me?

>LOIS
>Aren't you a private detective? Why not give someone I know the business instead of a stranger.

G-Man pulled out a Cuban cigar, lit it and began to puff. Then he sat back and sighed. He looked at the picture.

>G-MAN
>Lois, why do you need this man found?

>LOIS
>I'll pay you upfront if you stop asking me questions.

Lois pulled out her checkbook.

          G-MAN
Look, I'll find him, no charge to you--and you won't owe me.

Lois noticed a group of men enter the restaurant. One of the men was her husband.

          LOIS
Well looks like you won't need to find him. There he is right there.

Lois got up and went into the bathroom. The HUSBAND entered the restaurant with some of Gangsters' employees GH was among them.

          CRANE
Whassup Boss. Oh, I took care of that--and guess who I saw talking to Slick about some business. MC

          CRANE
Slick said they started a male escort service for extra money.

G-man motioned for Crane to sit and then he whispered something in his ear. He turned around and looked at HUSBAND, lowered his head and laughed. They both found the situation humorous. Soon the crowd left the eatery. Lois saw this and took her seat at the table.

          LOIS
What was so funny?

          G-MAN
Nothing Lois, actually it's rather sad you were willing to pay me to go look for that man. I've been knowing him for 15 years. We were pretty cool back in the day. I swear I hadn't even recognized him from the picture. He looks good, though. I see why you're trying to find him. Why'd you leave when he came in. You don't want to be seen with me?

          LOIS
That's not it. I didn't want to have to say anything to him. I don't like scenes.

          G-MAN

> I hear you on that.

G-Man looked out of the window at Tunks. Then back a Lois, who was shoveling huge chunks of ravioli into her mouth.

INSIDE MC'S OFFICE-DAY:

In-law sends a call back to MC

>> MC
> Yes, how can I help you G-man?

>> G-MAN
> I need to stop by your office tonight to discuss a little business--and I'll be bringing Slick with me.

>> MC
> Alright, see you about six.

>> G-MAN
> By the way, why don't you sweep your office for bugs before we get there? I hear you got some problems with the government.

>> MC
> Why don't we just meet at Slick's about six, instead. It might be safer that way.

Gangster hung up the phone.

INT: SLICK'S MIRAGE-NIGHT

The parking lot was empty when MC arrived except for G-man's huge SUV. Tunks is parked two blocks away.

When Martin enters the club it is quiet. Slick and G-Man are seated in a booth. As MC approaches the table he sees G-Man take out a 9mm semi-automatic pistol and place it on the table.

>> MC
> What's this meeting supposed to do for us here?

>> G-man
> Well, for me, it will set us all straight. We won't have to become unsettled with each other.

SLICK
We might as well be upfront because we all have a lot to lose if we're not careful.

MC
Slick, you know what kind of position I'm in. You know how all of this started--as a joke or something. Now, there are people lurking outside of my home, the case is being investigated...

MC sits down with the men and they are all quiet for a moment.

MC
G-man, are those boys your sons? Lois and I had a little conversation about what is going on...

G-MAN
Yes. Look, I hired you because I heard you were good. And I expect you to pull this off. Slick told me about the service you have been providing. Believe it or not, that was my idea. I told Herra when we used to kick it back in the day.

MC looks at G-man for a moment.

G-MAN
Man, don't eyeball me. I knew that woman back when, see. She's not new to me but I was surprised to see Herra with you.

MC
I helped her negotiate a few contracts a while back.

G-Man puts his weapon back inside his jacket.

G-MAN
When was the last time you heard from Herra?

MC
I don't know, it's been a while

G-MAN
I sent her ass back to Hollywood. I got her a movie deal. And I guess she got someone else to help her with her contracts--so don't call or bother her in

anyway. Let her be.

>   SLICK
> At this point MC, all you have to do is win the
> case. Nothing gets personal here--it's too crucial.

Slick signals to the bartender to bring them a round of whiskey.

>   SLICK
> I'm not going to lose this club. I'm legit now, and
> I'd like to keep it that way.

>   MC
> A few things have been cleared up for me. But I
> don't see why the boys were arrested.

>   G-MAN
> Look, both of the children are mine. Gina is Luke's
> mother and Tony's mom died of a drug overdose when
> he was three days old. I don't answer to anyone and
> I'm not selfish but I'm not a punk either. Even I
> can only do so much by myself.

G-Man stands up and starts to leave the booth.

>   G-MAN
> Mc, had I told you straight out to represent my
> children, would you have accepted the case?

Mc lowered his head and swirled his whisky around his glass. He takes a sip. He didn't answer the man.

>   G-MAN
> That's what I thought. How can I explain to a
> complete stranger how a cop who got fired ten years
> ago for trying to shake me down, still has a really
> big hair up his ass. Tunks is crazy. So he took it
> out on my kids--and now you are the designated
> savior, MC.

>   MC
> This case would be much easier to win if some of
> these--people--were arrested or at least distracted.
> I got a call from Lois today. She said the FBI paid
> her editor a visit and now she, along with the rest
> of the news agencies in town should leave the case

alone. Stop writing about it.

Slick takes the liquor down in one quick gulp.

> G-MAN
> I think it would make the case easier to win but who's going to call the FBI.

> SLICK
> What if they just found out? Got hold to some evidence or something.

> G-MAN
> How are you going to do that without getting a whole lot of people killed--namely you. You need to stay alive. You have a lot of family to take care of.

> SLICK
> Shit. They're men just like we are. I got a few ideas.

MC leaves the club. Tunks gets out of his car, catching MC before he gets in his car.

> TUNKS
> Hey, take a look at this.

Tunks tosses MC a video tape and walks backwards back to his car. He gets in and drives away.

MC stands near his car, keys in hand. He doesn't get in for a moment. He leans his face on the roof of his car and sobs.

INT: MC'S CONDO-BEDROOM-NIGHT

MC pops the videotape into his VCR. The glow of the television reflects off of his face as his mouth contorts in horror at what is shown on the screen.

INSERT: BLACK AND WHITE VIDEO

A foggy closed circuit video, showcased the sexual athletics between himself and Herra. It showed them intertwined in his office and his home. He stopped the tape and then the phone rang.

> MC

>   Hello?

>   CROWE
> You should drop that case, MC.

The phone went dead. MC let it drop to the floor. He started to pack.

SERIES OF SHOTS

MC grabs five suits out of his closet

Sweeps toiletries into a shaving case.

Goes inside a wall safe and takes out a stack of money.

Grabs several hangers of shirts and ties out of the closet and throws it in a suitcase.

Slams the door to his car as he squeals away from his home in the middle of the night.

END SERIES

INT: LOIS' HOUSE

Lois who has recently moved out of her three-flat into a modest suburban split-level, is sitting in front of her fireplace, gliding her fingers across her keyboard, typing a magazine article. The phone rings.

>   LOIS
> Hey MC, what's up?

Lois checks her watch. It's 11:30 p.m.

>   MC
> I need to talk to you--in person.

>   LOIS
> Okay. You mean now?

>   MC
> Yeah, I'm parked outside your house.

Lois gets up, re-wraps her robe around her body and checks the window.

EXT: LOIS' HOUSE

MC is sitting in his car. He waves, Lois waves back and opens the door. MC grabs his bag and gets out of the car. He walks inside the house.

INT: LOIS' HOUSE

MC's eyes settle on an ashtray where a cigarette was burning, a baby bottle and a picture of Lois' husband on the fireplace mantle, all before he is able to put his bags down.

          MC
I didn't know you smoked.

Lois takes the bags and shuts the door.

INT: TUNK'S CAR

Crowe, Marrsec and Tunks are sitting in Tunk's car outside of the police station where he used to work. They're drinking beer.

          TUNKS
I'm going to get G-Man. I am.

          MARRSEC
They put the boys upstairs in an empty wing of the jail. It's nice--I mean for a jail.

          TUNKS
Don't start with that again. I don't want to hear it. This is the only way it can be done. He will respect me.

Crowe is sitting in the passenger's seat, sullen.

          CROWE
Tunks it's not like we planned this out or anything. And so far, I'm the one who has put it all on the line. All I ever see you do is--this.

Crowe motions with his hands indicating sitting in a car.

          TUNKS
You won't be saying that when I give you your cut. You'll have your mouth full of boobs or something.

The men laughed a little.

> MARRSEC
> Well, I hear the feds are looking at the case.

> TUNKS
> What wrong with that. The kids confessed, didn't they? You can't beat a confession of guilt. And you have two witnesses placing them at the scene of the crime.

> CROWE
> I don't know where those punks are. I went by their hangout, put the word out. There's no sign of them.

> TUNKS
> Even better then. No loose ends. You guys need to stop fretting so much. The guy's a criminal for God's sake. No one cares about what happens to him-- and the kids will survive. Hell, my old man beat the shit outta me until he died. Then I was shipped off to a foster home. They'll live.

INT: SLICK'S MIRAGE-OFFICE-NIGHT

Slick sits alone in his office with a bottle of Absolute Pepper Vodka sitting on his desk. He picks up his phone to call ANGELA, an old friend.

> SLICK
> Angela, I need you to return a favor for me. Can you meet me at the club in an hour?

Slick hangs up the phone.

INT: G-MAN'S OFFICE-DAY

G-Man goes into the warehouse with bags of fast food.

> G-MAN
> Here. You know, I'm getting tired of feeding you two.

> THUG 1
> Then let us go. We've been down here for a month.

> G-MAN
> No, it's only been a few days.

G-Man leaves the men to eat.

> **G-MAN**
> Remember to use the bucket.

He closes the door behind him as both men eat hungrily.

ACT III

INT: LOIS' HOUSE

Lois and MC are sitting across from each other on the floor near the fireplace.

> **MC**
> What are you writing about?

> **LOIS**
> I'm working on a magazine article about the two boys and how they came to be arrested. I figured if no one around hear was interested in the story, someone else might be.

> **MC**
> You don't give up, do you.

> **LOIS**
> No, not easily. Why should I? The story needs to be told and now I have someone willing to publish it.

Lois reaches for three glossy magazines and hands them to MC. He examines each one.

> **MC**
> These are fashion magazines.

> **LOIS**
> No, they're more than that.

Lois reaches over her laptop to point out the finer points of each publication.

INSERT--The magazines

HIP HOP DIARY

NEWS

THE ENVELOPE

Back to scene

As Lois flips furiously through HIP HOP DIARY, MC grabs her hand and attempts to pull her near but she draws away.

          LOIS
You're sleeping on the couch, MC

          MC
What's wrong?

          LOIS
Mc, you show up on my doorstep, bags in hand, and I let you stay here no questions asked--and no doubt you didn't offer an explanation.

MC drops the magazine and rolls over on his back, holding his head.

          MC
Lois, someone put a hidden camera in my home. And somehow they've taped me--all of me if you know what I mean.

Lois is silent. She picks up her pack of cigarettes and starts to smoke. Then she gets up and heads towards the refrigerator.

          LOIS
Wanna beer?

MC rolls over to see Lois sticking her head in the refrigerator.

          MC
Yeah, I'll take one.

          MC
Lois, I didn't know where else to go, considering the situation. I only need a place to stay for the night.

Lois returns to the living room with the beer.

          LOIS
It's not that MC--a place to stay--it's the romantic gesture. I mean, why initiate something like that. We're both in situations. And it's not that I don't want to.

Lois sits on the sofa and pours her beer in a glass. MC gets up and removes silk pajamas out of his bag.

          MC
It's comforting to know you want to too.

MC walks over to the sofa and plants a kiss on Lois' head before walking off to the bathroom. Lois sits on the couch with her head in her lap. Then she picks up one of the magazines and starts to fan herself with it.

G-MAN'S SUV-DAY

G-Man picks Slick up outside of the club.

          SLICK
I called a friend of mine last night and we got a plan together it should work.

          G-MAN
Whoa, who is your friend?

          SLICK
Angela. She's got connections in Washington D.C.

          G-MAN
What's the plan?

          SLICK
It seems they have a point man here in town. He's been here a year and a half, supposedly investigating corruption in the town. He's looking to retire soon and he's not with anyone.

          G-MAN
Yeah, so?

          SLICK
He's meeting with Angela today. She likes lonely old men nearing retirement.

G-Man doesn't respond, just looks at Slick.

> SLICK
> Now what you need to do is to let Tunks know you're ready to make a deal. This should make it a little easier for MC to get the charges dropped against the boys

> G-MAN
> Hold it. Make a deal with Tunks for what? I'm not giving him shit!

> SLICK
> Come on. I know you don't want to mess around with that stupid escort service. It wasn't even making any money. It was strictly for entertainment purposes only. Me and MC go back a-ways and it was good advertising for the club and all. All you have to do is let Tunks take that over. No telling who knows about it, so if Tunks happens to hook up a few undercover officers--well that's his problem.

G-Man, laughing, offers Slick one of his cigars.

> G-MAN
> When is all of this supposed to go down?

> SLICK
> As soon as you let Tunks know he's the man.

The men bounce happily down the street in the SUV puffing on cigars.

INT: HOTEL ROOM

Angela and Charley Huff have just had sex.

> ANGELA
> I've missed you. You used to call all of the time.

> CHARLEY
> I know, I got a little wrapped up in this case. It's been a struggle sifting through a town of liars. I swear, I have never seen so much unchecked corruption in my entire career. And I've been doing this three decades almost. Everybody's dirty.

ANGELA
When are you going wrap up this case. You need a vacation.

CHARLEY
As soon as I can pin down the top dog around here. I have couple of suspects.

ANGELA
If I help you pin down this monster, will you go away with me?

CHARLEY
Yeah, what do you know about this case?

ANGELA
I don't know for sure but I hear on the street an ex-cop is running a group of men and women--escorts, drugs and stuff.

CHARLEY
Honey, what I'm looking for is a little more than that.

ANGELA
I hear their bringing in all kinds of things--human cargo, drugs--everything goes. A friend of mine knows the ring leader. She said his name is Tunks.

CHARLEY
No, he's not the type. He couldn't pull it off. I know who you're talking about. He's an ex-cop. Hell, he can't even keep a job let alone run a major vice operation.

ANGELA
Well me and my girlfriends are going down by the docks to party later on tonight. He usually hangs out down there. They pay homeless people to help them smuggle the illegal aliens into those sweatshops down by the river. I hear the aliens bring the drugs with them. And then they put the women out on the street to trick.

CHARLEY
Cutting into your pocketbook, eh?

                ANGELA
        Damn right it is. I thought I had lost you to them
        too. Look, I don't know how far this little ring of
        theirs reaches, but it's hurting me something
        terrible. I've been reduced to getting my clients
        through them. Out-of-towners can be dangerous.

                CHARLEY
        Alright. I'll check it out--just for you, Ang. If
        it's a big enough bust we can get outta here in a
        couple of weeks. I hear Aruba's nice.

Angela squeals and throws her arms around Charley's neck.

INT: SECLUDED WAREHOUSE-DAY

G-Man has arranged for Tunks to meet him at the warehouse. Behind him are bricks of cocaine and stacks of money. There is a knock at the door. And Tunks is on the other side.

                TUNKS
        Well, what do you have for me?

                G-MAN
        This, and a list of the people who should report to
        you from now on. They pretty much regulate
        themselves but you need to know who owes you what
        and when you should get it. You need to meet Mr. Kane
        later on tonight, he's your supplier. And there's
        your money.

G-man kicks a large container across the floor to Tunks.

                G-MAN
        You can count it if you want but all I want in
        return is the two boys' freedom. Then I'm getting
        outta here. You're on your own.

                TUNKS
        Fair enough. I'll place a few phone calls get the
        boys processed--but I want you out of town tonight.
        Don't look back. We don't need you around here.

G-man walks towards the door.

               G-MAN
I hope you know what you're doing. Mr. Kane is
expecting a certain level of cooperation. I don't
want him to have to look for either of us--you know,
honor among thieves. I told him you had the right
connections.

               TUNKS
Why are you giving up all of a sudden?

               G-MAN
I want my boys back.

G-man leaves the warehouse, driving away in his SUV.

Intercut telephone conversation

               TUNKS
Yeah, it's done. Call the prosecutor's office and
tell them you lost the evidence.

               CROWE
They'll know what I'm talking about, right.

               TUNKS
They will. Oh and meet me down here as soon as you
can.

Back to scene

Tunks opens up the container and picks up a bundle of cash.

Intercut telephone conversation

               TUNKS
Farley, why don't you see to it that those boys are
released tonight, in time for dinner. Their dad's
coming to pick them up.

               FARLEY
What.

               TUNKS
Don't worry about it. It'll be a few hundred
thousand worth your while.

> FARLEY
> This is it after this, Tunks. I'm out of all of this.--for good.

Tunks hangs up the phone.

> TUNKS
> Good, more for me.

INT: LOIS' HOUSE

MC, swathed in silk, has his long limbs slung over Lois' sofa. She walks into the living room and watches him half in and half out of his pajamas. She silently kneels on the floor beside the sofa, watching his chest rise and fall rhythmically. Lois doesn't wake him but instead leans over him taking in the air he expels. She lowers her lips near his, lingering. MC stirs and rolls away from her.

> MC
> I told you we should have did it.

Lois smiles, covering her mouth to stifle a laugh.

> LOIS
> How long have you been awake?

> MC
> Long enough to realize we should have done something last night.

> LOIS
> I dreamed about you. I don't know why.

Lois placed her head on MC's bare chest and he smoothed her hair. They were silent.

> LOIS
> Sometimes, I just want to be near you, like this even if it's just for a little while.

Mc cups Lois' face in his hands and they share a long deep kiss. Lois races her hands over Mc's chest and around his neck, squeezing him. Then she breaks away from the embrace only to share a heady look of passion with him.

> MC

I know. I know we can't.

Mc sits upright on the couch and helps Lois to her feet.

> MC
> Let's just hang out today, you and me.

> LOIS
> Okay.

> MC
> We can go shopping or something. Whatever you want to do.

Lois curls up on the sofa next to MC.

> MC
> What was your dream about?

Lois kisses MC tenderly on his temple and down to his ear. She whispers.

> LOIS
> It's a secret.

MC and Lois start kissing again.

INT: HOTEL ROOM

Charley is sitting on the side of the bed he shared with Angela. He's on the phone and she's gathering their things.

> CHARLEY
> Okay, it's all set up. All we have to do is show up looking for some action, they'll do all of the rest.

> ANGELA
> Good. Now, let's go to the travel agency. I know someone there and we can get a good deal on a cruise to Cancun.

INT: LOIS' HOUSE

Lois is standing over MC with the phone in her hand and his pager in the other.

> LOIS

> I think you ought to take this. You left your pager in the bathroom.

MC looks at the pager and sees that his office is paging him. He accepts the phone from Lois and calls in.

He hangs up and looks over at Lois who is pouring coffee. She brings him a cup.

> LOIS
> Did you sleep well?

> MC
> Yeah, I did. Thanks.

MC and Lois sip on their coffee.

> MC
> I guess I was dreaming.

Lois gives MC a look.

> LOIS
> Well, what's on your agenda for today?

> MC
> Apparently, I have a meeting with the state prosecutors. There was a development in the case. They're dropping the charges and exonerating the boys.

> LOIS
> Oh my God. When did all of this happen?

> MC
> I'm not sure. I'm going in soon. You want to come with?

> LOIS
> Yeah, let me call in and file a brief. They have to let me write this one up.

Lois scurries off to her desk, typing while MC just lays on the couch looking bewildered while he drinks down his coffee.

> MC

Hey Lois.

        LOIS
Yeah.

        MC
Do you snore?

Lois only turns around and gives him a look. She picks up the phone and talks with a spokesperson with the state prosecutor's office. She hangs up.

Insert: e-mail text on the new development

State prosecutors, in an astounding move, dropped all charges Friday against two boys who were charged with the murder of (Toyman). The children's attorney, Martin Combs, said Friday

        LOIS
No, but you do. That sofa's pretty comfortable, huh?

        MC
Yeah. By the way I need to get on the web when you're done. I gotta sweep my apartment for that hidden camera.

        LOIS
How are you going to do that? Hey--do you have any comments on the newest development in the case?

        MC
Yeah, I never lost faith in the integrity of our justice system and knew the evidence would find my clients innocent of all charges...

Lois finishes filing her story, calls her editor leaving a short message then hangs up.

        LOIS
I can tag along today, right?

        MC
Yeah, no doubt. Make sure you get a photographer there.

MC walks over to Lois and pulls up a chair besides her at the computer.

> MC
> I didn't know you used
> (that internet provider)
> I use the same one.

Lois logs on to the web and while they wait for the browser to pop up, they share a quick brush lightly of the hand. MC touches his lips to her neck and then kisses it lightly moving up to her face. Lois leans into the embrace and they actually kiss.

> LOIS
> Is this what your dream was about?

MC leans back in his chair, satisfied.

> MC
> I'm not telling you about my dream. It's for grown folks.

> LOIS
> Excuse me, sir--I'm about as grown as it gets around here.

MC leans in for another kiss but suddenly Lois turns her head towards the faint waking cry of her little girl, CARMEN. She gets up to see about her. MC sighs. He places his mug of coffee next to Lois' on the desk then moves over to Lois' seat and searches for the information he needs on the web..

INT: SLICKS' CAR T

Slick and G-Man are seated in Slick's car about a half-mile away from the warehouse. They keep tabs on the area with binoculars. Slick is looking through he binoculars.

> G-MAN
> I guess this how cops feel. Sitting in a car for half-a-day.

> G-MAN
> I see Tunks. I hope he knows what he is doing.

Insert binocular view:

Tunks, now dressed in leather and surrounded by a few other mob types, is entertaining Mr. Kane and his associates.

They are toasting.

Back to scene

Slick and G-Man are still staking out the warehouse.

        SLICK
I can't believe he fell for this shit.

        G-MAN
Me neither. I'm just glad he did. He wanted to live my life, so here it is. Getting busted, avoiding prison, fucked up life--lots of money, though.

        SLICK
Too bad you can't enjoy it.

        G-MAN
I even gave him the bank accounts.

        SLICK
You did all of this for your kids man. I never expected to see this side of you.

G-man gives Slick a side look and takes the binoculars from Slick. He looks through them.

INT: SECLUDED WAREHOUSE-NIGHT

        TUNKS
Gentlemen, to long life and good business.

The men raise their glasses. One of Mr. Kane's associates is holding a briefcase and the men are initiating a sale.

INT: SLICK'S CAR

G-man is still looking through the binoculars.

        G-MAN
That's not Mr. Kane. Drive around a little.

        SLICK
Damn this fool about to be busted.

The car slowly moves closer.

> G-MAN
> I don't know who those people are but they're not the people I know.

INT: SECLUDED WAREHOUSE-NIGHT

Tunks and Mr. Kane are making an exchange of money and drugs.

> TUNKS
> It's been nice working with you Mr. Kane but this is our one and final deal because I have other suppliers with better products. My friends will see your group out.

Tunks and Mr. Kane move towards the door of the warehouse. Tunks opens the door and the men file out quietly.

> MR. KANE
> You will regret this, Tunks.

> TUNKS
> Whatever.

Tunks slams the door shut. He and his associates start to celebrate for a short while but then there is a knock at the door. One of Tunks' men answers with his gun drawn as another looks by. He opens the door and is staring into the headlights of a huge military vehicle which surges forward, ramming the front wall of the warehouse and crushing several people.

Nearly 300 agents dressed in tactical gear rush through the rubble, arresting Tunks and the men who are left alive.

Mr. Kane gets out of vehicle as Tunks is being dragged away.

> MR. KANE
> Any regrets, Tunks?

> TUNKS
> Fuck you. I ain't no drug dealer. I was set up. That fuck G-Man is the one, not me. Fuck you.

Tunks is dragged into an unmarked squad screaming.

Several of the agents yell for assistance. They bring out, thin, dirty and weak, Thug 1 and Thug 2 and load them into a waiting ambulance.

INT: SLICK'S CAR

G-man is still looking through the binoculars.

> SLICK
> How much did this cost you?

> G-MAN
> Half. I figure the government finally got theirs and I got that fool off of my back. My kids are free.

> SLICK
> What will you do now.

G-man puts down the binoculars.

> G-MAN
> I guess I don't need you to do that little thing anymore if that's what you're getting at.

> SLICK
> Yeah, thanks man. I kinda figured that. But what are you going to do, now that you're retired?

> G-MAN
> Nothing, I guess. Buy a house somewhere maybe watch some television, spend some time with my boys. I had a good run, so I guess it's time to be Gerald Manning again.

G-man lights a cigar and surveys the contents of Slick's car which is filled with empty soda cans, food wrappers and assorted surveillance equipment.

> G-MAN
> Maybe I can be a cop. This was pretty cool.

> SLICK
> Okay, let's go man, I gotta club to run.

The men quietly drive away.

ONE YEAR LATER

Insert: Banner reads: Chronicle-Post

Front page byline: written by Lois DuSol.

Headline reads: DIRTY EX-COP GETS ONE YEAR

INT: LOIS' OFFICE:

Lois is holding the newspaper in one hand and cradling the phone chatting, while her new employee, Frank.

          LOIS
How many reporters do we still need to hire.

          FRANK
Well, I think three will do. We have a pretty full house but we can always use a good reporter.

MC enters the office.

          LOIS
Ready?

Frank stands up and excuses himself.

          MC
Yeah. I thought I told you I didn't want any press on this?

          LOIS
A story is a story. Anyway, who cares. He only got a year and you made your money. It's remarkable that you ended up defending the man who almost got us killed. I'm sorry bud, but that's a story.

          MC
So you don't mind that new gossip columnist you hired writing about you dating the man who defended the man, who almost got us killed.

          LOIS
MC, now you know I don't hire fools.

The pair kisses and moves towards the door.

          LOIS

I'll make it up to you this weekend. Did you call Gerald?

  MC
Yeah. House arrest has done him some good.

  LOIS
I'm sure. A lot of us wouldn't mind house arrest on our own private island--you picked up the tickets, right?

  MC
Yes I did. Momma was glad to watch Carmen for us. This should be a good time for all of the girls to get to know one another a little better.

  LOIS
Yeah. It's working out. Finally everything is working out. Everyone in our world is finally happy. Sometimes it's hard for me to accept so much joy. I'm not used to it.

  MC
I know. I swear Lois' who'd ever think that Gerald would end up doing all of this--legitimately.

  LOIS
That's how I avoid psychotherapy, Martin. I try not to think about it. I'm only trying to enjoy it.

Fade to black.

www.ingramcontent.com/pod-product-compliance
Ingram Content Group UK Ltd.
Pitfield, Milton Keynes, MK11 3LW, UK
UKHW050414240426
12048UKWH00020B/1509